STILL SHEISTY

Compilation and Introduction copyright © 2004 by
Triple Crown Publications
2959 Stelzer Rd., Suite C
Columbus, Ohio 43219
www.TripleCrownPublications.com

Library of Congress Control Number: 2004115364
ISBN# 0-9762349-0-4
Cover Design/Graphics: www.MarionDesigns.com
Editor: Chloé A Hilliard
Consulting: Vickie M. Stringer

First Trade Paperback Edition Printing November 2004

Printed in the United States of America

DEDICATION

To my daughter Tiana, I love you.

ACKNOWLEDGEMENTS

Thank you Jesus, for giving me the strength to complete my second book. With you, I know any and everything is possible.

To my editor, Chloé A. Hilliard, girl, I think you are just WONDERFUL! I feel fortunate to have had the opportunity to work with someone who listens, takes the time to explain, shows interests and makes herself available to me at all times. To me it don't get no better than that! I thank you so much.

To my mother Audrien Cox, Ma, I thank you for never leaving home without a flyer for Sheisty. Your support means the world to me I love you!

I would like to take all my loved ones names from Sheisty's acknowledgements and place them here. Unfortunately I can't, but everybody knows who they are and what they mean to me. The love is still the same. I would like to thank all my family on my fathers' side. I feel whole now that I have you guys in my life. Aunt Cleo, Uncle Sherman and all my cousins a.k.a The Fabulous Baker Boys and Girls. I love you guys. Let's keep in touch. To my good friend Michelle Jackson, thanks for always lending an ear when I need one and for the great advice, also. You are a beautiful person in and out. - Love Neish!

To my friend Liz, I got nothing but love for you baby. To Richard Holland, your friendship is a very special one to me. Thanks for all the pep talks and encouragement you've given me. Love ya!

To my publisher, Vickie Stringer, thanks for being patient with the completion of Still Sheisty and for showing me the love.

To all my TCP Family, much love and success. Keeping doing the damn thing.

Special thanks to Ka Shamba for keeping me informed with dates for all the book signings. Shannon Holmes, I'm glad were cool, now. Al-Saadiq Banks, thanks for the advice when I was going through tough times in this business. I wish you much success.

Special thanks to Masamba on Jamaica Ave. for supporting Sheisty. Keep pushing those copies. Much love. And to **all the readers that supported Sheisty...I thank you for the bottom of my heart**. Big Tone...you know I love you, right? I also thank everybody that I might have forgot who play a part in my life, it's not intentional so please don't take it personal.

PROLOGUE

Epiphany

"I closed my eyes and squeezed the trigger. Not knowing whether or not my shot was a successful one. I felt a burning sensation pierce through my chest. "Noooooo," I screamed as I was thrown to the floor from the strong impact. Instantly I could feel the warmth of my blood leaking from the stinging wound. My eyes started getting heavy. The pain was too much to bear............

Keisha

I opened the door to my bedroom and right away tears started to fill my eyes as I watched Tucker sitting on the edge of the bed watching the video tape from my bacholorette party............

Shana

I followed Smitty to the door on his way out and before I could thank him for covering my ass he turned to me with a devious smirk and said, 'You owe me nigga!' From his look alone I knew I was in for the bullshit.

Triple Crown Publications presents

CHAPTER ONE

"Oh god, please noooooo-," were the last words Epiphany whispered as tears fell down the sides of her face and she lost consciousness after the shooting. C-God damn near pissed himself; his heart pounded rapidly. For a moment he thought *he* was shot. Fortunately for him, Epiphany's aim was way off because she closed her eyes when she squeezed the trigger.

"Yo man, c'mon we gotta get the fuck up out of here," Ness screamed. C kneeled down beside Epiphany and felt remorseful. Finally, he felt her pain. In any other situation he wouldn't have given a fuck, especially when it came down to his life. But this wasn't just any situation and as much as he tried to front on Epiphany, he really did care for her. He had no intentions on killing her. He just wanted to shake her up enough to get her to talk. C-God looked down at the papers still clutched in his hand, confirming Epiphany's pregnancy and felt even more fucked up.

"Yo, fuck that bitch. Lets role, dawg!" Ness yelled in a panic. Finally, C snapped out of it, grabbed both guns and together they fled the scene doing eighty down South Jamaica's residential back streets.

"Nigga you must of been soft on that chick, but yo it was either you or her nigga, look at it that way." Ness was the type of nigga with a big ass mouth that didn't know how to leave well enough alone. "If I ain't come up in there when I did, your shorty might of murked you dawg, for real, but I had your back though."

C-God just sat there wearing a screw faced look on his face, thinking about the 'what ifs' as he listened to Ness in silence. Deep down C- God knew Epiphany would have kept shooting at him until she killed him. So yes, he felt Ness reacted the way he was supposed to when he shot her, but C didn't want to hear him boasting about it. Obviously the look on his face wasn't enough because Ness didn't catch the hint; he just continued to go on and on about the incident until suddenly C snapped.

"Shut the fuck up, damn! A nigga can't even think straight, with you running the fuck off at the mouth. Just don't say shit else to me until I ask you to and pull this muthafucka over at that payphone right there."

Ness did what he was told – shut the fuck up and pulled over. It was C-God's duty to live his life coldheartedly. He never cared too much about anybody, except his parents. Outside of them the rest of his family was cool but if they crossed him they could easily be killed for doing so. But on the real he was all bark with no bite, only nobody knew it because they never put him to the test. It was his older brothers that were the truth back in the days. Nigga's ain't fuck with his three brothers or whoever they considered to be family. Pop, Black Russ and Lloyd were well-known and now 'legendary gangstas', ranking with some of the best that ever terrorized Queens. They were ruthless with no respect for a person's life, killers without a cause. If they weren't feeling you for whatever reason, then they didn't give a fuck about you or your family and in their presence you better had shown fear. Unfortunately, living that life came back to haunt them, leading to Pop and Russ's brutal deaths and landing Lloyd in prison for life with no chance of parole. Still, C-God felt since he was the last breed of the notorious Hinderson brothers he had something to prove. He had to own up to his family name and the reputation they paved. For some reason, his conscious was eating away at him tonight and that ain't supposed to happen to no Hinderson.

C-God picked up the receiver on the pay phone using the papers he took from Epiphany's purse and with a piece of tissue covering his fingertip, he dialed the police. He always thought with a criminals mind. Disguising his voice in an unrecognizable high-pitched tone he called for an ambulance in hopes that Epiphany might still be alive.

Epiphany briefly regained consciousness, oblivious to the sounds of the loud sirens as she lied still in a pool of her own blood. An ambulance and three police cars arrived at the scene shortly after the call was made. The cops entered first and took a look around, then signaled the paramedics with an 'okay, the coast was clear'. When the paramedics entered, the police suggested they tend to the girl first, besides from the looks of things it was obvious that Malikai was already deceased. The EMS workers immediately ran over to Epiphany and checked her vital signs.

"She's still alive," one of them shouted. "Start an IV, her pulse is weak, this is not good. She's losing a lot of blood. Let's get a move on it fast!" Lifting Epiphany onto the stretcher he continued, "We're losing her; let's get her to the hospital now!"

Triple Crown Publications presents

CHAPTER TWO

Keisha stood in the bedroom doorway completely appalled. Her heart fell into the pit of her stomach and tears instantly fell down her face. As she stood there, her fiancé watch her give herself to another man—performing and receiving sexual pleasures on camera as if her name was Janet Jackme. She froze; stuck on stupid, puzzled as to how the videotape she destroyed managed to resurface again. She searched for the right words to say. She wanted to say something, but what? *"I'm sorry."* No, that wasn't gonna cut it. There was nothing to be said. She fucked up and she knew it. She felt like she had just slid down a razor blade, right into a pool of alcohol. Tucker's face was filled with a rage that she had never seen before. A rage that put fear in Keisha's heart. She was afraid to say or do anything so she continued to watch him watch her fuck and suck on another man in ways she had never done with him since they'd been together. He never ever thought about putting his hands on any women, let alone Keisha, until now. Fuming, he was to the point were he really wanted to hurt her. Tucker jumped up, snatched the VCR from the top of the 52" screen TV and frisbeed it into to the wall close to were Keisha was standing. Keisha jumped out of the way and into the hallway as the VCR crashed into the wall and then hit the floor.

Water flooded his eyes and his heart was filled with pain. This was the ultimate feeling of betrayal, but he would never give her the satisfaction of seeing him cry. No one for that matter. His militant father instilled in him as a boy that a man ain't supposed to cry. A strong man sucks it all up and keeps it moving. By now, all types of distasteful thoughts ran through Tucker's mind, but he never said a word. He simply looked at Keisha with such anger and disgust. If looks could kill she would have suffered a painful death. Keisha was still standing in the hall, afraid to move or say a word. She wasn't sure what to expect from this furious side of Tucker. Keisha's mother, Loretta, and her son, lil' T, were awakened and startled when they heard the crashing sound. She jumped out of bed, grabbed the baby and rushed from the bedroom to see what was going on. Right outside her door she spotted Keisha near the doorway of her bedroom crying.

"Keisha is everything okay," asked her concerned mother. Keisha didn't respond, instead she took it as an opportunity to get out of Tucker's sight. Making a run for the bathroom she locked herself inside and cried like a baby. Loretta was curious as to what was going on. She assumed that maybe it was just a heated discussion about the wedding postponement. Since there wasn't any sign of domestic violence she felt no need to get involved, so she headed back to her room. Tucker had no sympathy for Keisha or her tears and at this point, all he felt for her was pure hatred, but he would never hurt her because of his son.

'Let me just get the fuck up out of here,' he said to himself, quickly gathered up some of his belongings and broking out in a hurry. He wasn't sure if his anger would allow him to honor the fact that she was his baby's mother. Once the sound of Tucker's truck sped off, confirming that the coast was now clear, Loretta laid Lil' T in the bed and came back out of her room. She knocked gently on the bathroom door.

"Keisha is everything alright?" She whispered again.

Keisha wasn't alright, her life was over. She opened the door and fell into her mother's arms for comfort.

"He's gone and I don't think he's coming back." Keisha stuttered as she cried.

"What happened?"

"The tape, he saw the tape."

"No! Keisha, how? I thought you got rid of it."

"I did, I did. And there's no way possible, that could be the same tape. Somebody had to set me up. One of the girls at my bachelorette party, posing to be my friend, set this whole thing up and my stupid ass fell for it. Now he's gone and what am I gonna do, huh? How am I ever gonna get Tucker to forgive me?" She asked her mother, hoping and wishing she could give her all the right answers.

"Keisha, you know Tucker loves you, just give him some time. He'll come around so you guys can at least talk and try to work things out. In the meantime, you need to be strong and try to keep it together, not only for you, but for that baby boy in the next room. Don't make the same mistakes that I did. You know what you did was wrong, but we all make mistakes. I know you love him and he knows it too. Understand that that was a pretty big bomb you dropped on him, so he's gotta be devastated and full of hurt right now. You' re the mother of his son, a son that he loves more than anything in this world and nothing will ever change that. Just give it some time, he'll come around. You just have to pray for the best and prepare for the worst just in case he can't find it in his heart to forgive you. If he can't, then you just got to find a way to move on." Loretta said stroking her daughter's head while she cried in her arms.

Keisha listened to her mother's words, but at the same time she didn't feel like she could manage life without Tucker. She went and got her son from her mother's bed. Holding him close, she reminisced on how happy Tucker was when she told him she was pregnant. Their son, lil' man, was the bond that she and Tucker shared; a bond created out of love. A bond that because of her stupidity might be the only thing she has left of Tucker. Before shutting her puffy red eyes and get some sleep, she made a promise to herself to find out which one of those bitches was responsible for causing this misery.

CHAPTER THREE

Epiphany's father had a terrible ringing in his left ear all evening. Old folks used to say that when you heard a ringing sound in your ear that was the sound of death bells and someone close to you was gonna die. Jay Wright didn't believe that ol' superstitious shit, but for some reason tonight's feeling just wasn't right. Those feeling were confirmed when he was awakened in the middle of the night by the doorbell. He jump up out of bed and rushed down the stairs to see who it was. It had to be some bad news 'cause nobody rang his bell that time of morning since he left the drug game three years ago. When he reached the door, he opened it slightly and peaked out to find two police officers, one black and one white, standing there. He assumed something might of happened to his brother Ramel, who took over his position when he retired from the game. Before he could speak one of the officers addressed him.

"Good morning Sir, I'm officer Johnson and this is officer Riley we're sorry to bother you at this time of morning, but are you Jay Wright?"

Epiphany's dad hated the police, but he kept his composure because finding out their reason for being at his front door was more important.

"Yes officer, I am. What's going on?"

"Mr. Wright, I'm sorry to have to be the bearer of bad news, but your daughter Epiphany and a young man were found shot in her apartment around midnight. The man was pronounced dead at the scene. Your daughter was severely wounded and rushed to the nearest hospital. We don't know the status of her condition but she was still alive when she was admitted to the hospital."

"AWW FUCK! FUCK HELL NAH ! NAH, NOT EPEE!" Jay Wright punched his fist through the wooden door. His wife awakened from her sound sleep when she heard his loud outburst. She threw on her robe and came running down the stairs. Hearing her husband yell out like that could only mean that something terrible had happened.

"Baby what is it? What's wrong? Oh my god, baby what happened?" She questioned with fear. Jay's face said it all. She knew something was terribly wrong and her gut instincts told her it was Epiphany. She started to cry. "Where is she Jay? What happened to Epee? Jay answer me. Please say she's alright!" She demanded frantically.

"Baby listen, we gotta go to the hospital. Epee's been hurt" he said grabbing her close trying to comfort her. He knew any second she was about to lose it.

"No, no, no, not my child. Where is she Jay? What happened? What fucking hospital, huh?" She cried out and tussled to break from his arm lock.

"Stop it Tiara, you gotta calm down. She's been shot. Now either you gon' sit here and go crazy, or go get your shit so we can go see about her," he said putting the situation in a better perspective. The police offered to take them to the hospital, but Jay refused. Before he could slam the door shut the officer handed him his card and informed him that he might have to answer some questions later. They wanted to know if he had any idea who might have wanted to harm his daughter or the young man that was with her.

"Yo, I'on know nothing right now, but whoever did this better hope you guys find 'em before I do. Now will that be all," Jay said fuming.

"Mr. Wright, I know your upset, but trust that we'll do the best that we can to find the shooter or shooters. I can only imagine how you must be feeling because if that was my little girl lying up in some hospital bed with a gun shot wound to the chest, badly beaten and barely holding on, I'd want to take matters into my own hands too. But you take it easy you hear" said the Uncle Tom officer Johnson. Both police officers turned to walk away. Once they reached the squad car Riley looked at his partner with a devilish smirk on his face.

"Hey Johnson, what was that about? You damn near told the man to take the law into his own hands."

"That's exactly what I did. I could tell you some stories about that man. Mr. J. 'Smooth Criminal' Wright aka *'The Untouchable'*. He was big time, some years ago. The State and the Feds had him under investigation for years, but we could never get any hard evidence on that nigger to arrest or convict him, not even a petty crime. He knew the game well; too well. So, I was just giving the brother a little rope to hang himself with, if you know what I mean. A little encouragement never hurt nobody. Besides, knowing that scum like him is behind bars would help a lot of us sleep better at night," he laughed.

"Maybe what happen to his daughter was someone settling the score, or having vendetta against him," said Riley.

"Yeah, could be, unless the apple doesn't fall far from the tree and she got herself caught up in her own mess. We'll just sit on this one, push it to the side, and let the animals do what they do best- *kill each other off*," said Smith.

Jay Wright wasted no time getting to the hospital, doing a 110mph on the Van Wyck Expressway. Under any other circumstances, Epiphany's mom would have been car sick from that type of speed, but this time was different.

"Hurry, Jay, hurry," she hollered. They arrived at the Hospital in five minutes flat. Jay pulled up to the front of the emergency entrance. Both of them hopped out of car and rushed through the double door entrance of the emergency waiting room.

"Sir, excuse me you can't park there," said the flashlight security guard. Jay pushed pasted the guard. Right now, his only concern was his daughter and finding out her condition. Then, he wanted the bastards responsible for trying to kill her, even if he had to take shit back to the old school way of handling beef.

"Excuse me Miss, we're looking for our daughter, Epiphany Wright. She was shot and brought in by an ambulance a couple of hours ago. Can you tell me where we can find her please?" Tiara said to the lady behind the information desk. The lady punched Epiphany's name into the keyboard and directed them to the Intensive Care Unit. Once they reached the ICU, they still had to follow the same procedure again.

"Excuse me, I was told that we could find our daughter here. Her name is Epiphany Wright, she's twenty-two years old and she was shot," said her father, this time getting even more impatient and hoping that she could assist them. Before the nurse could answer any questions the doctor walked up.

"Excuse me, I'm Doctor Frye, did I over hear you asking about a young woman that was shot? Are you her parents?"

"Yes we are, is she okay Doctor?" Tiara asked.

"Come with me please," the doctor said. "It's been a long morning." Doctor Frye let out a sigh as the three of them began walking down the corridor. "Your daughter was shot with a .38, which is a very powerful gun, in the chest. When she was brought in she had already lost an enormous amount of blood. We had to rush her into surgery right away. Her heart rate was fading fast and we were without a doubt going to losing her. I had no choice but to authorize an emergency transfusion to get her heart to start pumping again. It was successful. She also has a ruptured lung that I was able to save. That's the good news. The bad news is the baby your daughter was carrying did not make it.

"BABY! Wait a minute, what baby?" Her mother was shocked.

"Yes, your daughter was in the very, very early stage of her first trimester. Unfortunately, she lost a lot blood so the oxygen supply to the baby was cut off. Your daughter apparently miscarried before she even got to the hospital." Tiara's jaw dropped. Jay Wright wrapped his arm around is wife but couldn't bear to look at her. "Also I noticed a lot of bruises on her body, which leads me to believe that whoever shot her had beaten her first. That could've been the initial cause of the miscarriage. Either way, the child would not have survived. As of now your daughter's condition is still critical, she's in a coma and due to her injuries she's on a respirator. Your daughter is definitely a fighter and I strongly believe she will pull through this. She's in room 202 right down here to your left."

Triple Crown Publications presents

CHAPTER FOUR

On his way to the hotel he'd been staying at for the past week or so, Tucker tried calling Malikai's cellphone several times, but didn't get an answer. He figured Malikai probably got caught up with Epiphany all over again. Even though Mali never told him, Tucker knew his boy was still sprung the fuck out over her conceited ass. But right now, he could've used some of his boy's advice. Malikai has been there for him from day one; before the money, cars and even Keisha. So, his feedback about what Tucker should do about the situation with Keisha, the videotape and the nigga she was fucking on it, was needed. There was no doubt that he still loved Keisha with all his heart, but at that moment he wished her dead. Mali would understand and never sugarcoat anything just to spare his best friend's feelings; he would give it to him raw and be honest about it. Once he got to his room he plopped down on the bed and stared at the ceiling until he finally fell asleep. At about six in the morning, Tucker's cell phone and two-way started going off like crazy. He ignored the first few rings, assuming it was Keisha ready to plead her case, but after tossing and turning to the vibrating sound of his two-way and the constant ringing of his cell, he became annoyed and finally went to answer his phone. The caller id said Momma D.

'*Maybe the nigga stayed at his Mother's house last night,*' he thought picked up the cell. He heard the unbearable sounds of a mother's cry. His heart ached instantly. Afraid of the possibilities, he hesitated for a moment.

"Momma D, what is it, what's wrong?"

"O lawd, lawd, lawd, my son is gone, he's dead Tucker. Malikai is dead. The police came and wanted me to go identify his body. But I just can't. Tucker what I'ma do now—my only boy is gone—what I'ma do?" She asked.

Tucker was crushed. *'This can't be'* he thought. There was nothing he could say or do that would ease Mrs. McKenzie's pain.

"Momma D, get dress! I'm on my way to get you," was all he said before ending the call. In disbelief he called Mali's cell repeatedly and got the voicemail each time just like he did when he tried to reach him last night.

"Nah, Mali not you dawg." Tucker mumbled.

Malikai wasn't only a business partner to Tucker, he was like his own flesh and blood—the only nigga he could trust with his life, money, girl and his kid. Mali trusted him just the same. He was a genuine dude. Tucker knew this for a fact because he tested his loyalty on several occasions and Malikai passed every time with flying colors. He was alone in this world, for real now. He got up out of the hotel bed, got dress and headed over to Momma D 's house. She opened the door wearing a wrinkled dress, mixed matched shoes and her wig was on crooked. She was an emotional wreck. Tucker didn't know what else to do beside wrap his arms tightly around Momma D to console her.

"Momma D, come on we gotta go do this, maybe it ain't him," Tucker said trying to be hopeful for the both of them.

"No Tucker, I...I can't go see my son lying dead on some cold metal table with his brains all over the place. I just can't and I won't. The police already showed me his picture anyway. I know it's him. The streets done took my son from me; this cruel world done killed him. All I had left is gone. I just buried my husband two years ago and now I gotta bury my son. No, you go for me Tucker, you were like a brother to him and I can't see my boy looking like that, I just can't."

Mrs. Delores had always been like a mother to Tucker, especially ever since his moms past away when he was eleven. She never treated him as anything less than a son and he depended on her for the motherly love she gave to him. She was such a sweet old lady, the type that would feed you a good hot meal if you were hungry and give you half of her last dollar if you needed it. Tucker had mad love and respect for her. He even gave her the nicknames Momma D and Mom Dukes— both short for Delores, her first name. So, to see her suffering caused Tucker a great deal of pain. He planted a kiss on her forehead and headed for the morgue. On his way there, it was so ironic that Puffy's tribute to Biggie, *'I'll be missing you,'* was playing on the radio. Tucker refused to believe it until he saw him. He phoned his boys from the Dirty South, Peewee and Cornell, to tell them the news. Everything became a reality when he stepped into the morgue. Tucker's body caught an instant chill from the cool temperature in the place and the smell of dead people gave him a nauseating feeling. The coroner asked him what his relationship was to the deceased.

"I'm his brother." Tucker followed the man to another room where he saw his best friend lying dead with a head the size of a basketball and his brains oozing out on the table. His stomach felt very weak from the sight of Malikai and his emotions were mixed with pain, anger and sorrow. Mali was the closest thing to a brother he had and his loss was too great to ignore. Tucker disregarded the words of his father and shed a few tears. Then he started to beat up on himself, feeling responsible for not being there to protect Malikai. He failed as his brother's keeper. To him, he was just as much the blame as the nigga that pulled the trigger. Looking at Malikai lying there like that was hard on his eyes. Tucker leaned over Mali's corpse and thought about all the good times they shared, there were so many memories to hold on to. Malikai, twenty-five, was too young to die, he was just starting to live life and just like that, it was over.

"Damn Mali, we should have left this drug game alone along time ago. It's over for me now. This shit is so played out, I'm done! I don't want to do this shit no more." Tucker spoke to

Malikai as if he could hear him. The shine was no longer worth the headache, heartache, or losses that come along with the territory. Tucker was eighteen when he started selling drugs and it took him every bit of the ten years he spent hustling to realize that this game ain't fair. It's a lot of money to be made, but it'll never make you rich nor will it let you go without paying a price. Either you lose yourself, your freedom or your soul at the end of either road, it ain't worth it. Tucker would never gain anything from hustling that could replace his loss, so for him this *was* the end of the road. Malikai's death was surely his wake up call, while he still had half a soul left. The game, as he knew it, was over.

CHAPTER FIVE

Shana couldn't help but wonder what Smitty's *"you owe me"* comment meant as he walked out the door. She didn't spend too much time dwelling on it 'cause more then anything else, she was happy he finally left her and K.C. alone. Shana wasted no time taking advantage of her *'alone at last'* thoughts as soon as she closed the door behind Smitty. Her man was home from jail and it was time to put some good ol' *'freedom pussy'* on his ass. For the past couple of months she'd been giving it to him with restrictions due to the rules of their conjugal visits. Shana fucked K.C. until his nut sack started running on empty, putting him into a comatose sleep for the rest of the night. That was a good move on her part because shortly after that the phone started to ring off the hook. It was Chasity calling just to harass her. Shana decided to pick up and hear her out but all she would say was, *"bitch,"* and then hang up so Shana turned off the ringer. Still, she couldn't sleep, thinking about the stunt Chasity had pulled earlier - the crank calls and wondering how much further she was gonna take things.

'I swear if I would of known the girl was a psycho I would of never fuck around with her.' She also thought about Smitty coming to her rescue with the quick cover up. That was real suspect, to her because her vibes for Smitty weren't right from day one. She could tell he was a sheisty individual. Being from the streets, where game recognize game, it ain't hard to tell whose grimey off of one sit down conversation. Smitty fit the bill in every sense

19

of the word, so when he said she owed him; he meant it because it wasn't in his character to lookout for her for nothing. Without any doubt, Shana knew he had some shit up his sleeve. She just didn't know what to expect.

'Maybe I should have just been straight up with K.C. about what went down while he was locked up.' Shana never thought his life-sentence would really get thrown out, so she kept her secret to herself. Now, she had to make sure Smitty kept it. K.C. had issues with the fact that his mom was a lesbian. It was because of that, she knew it would matter that she had been with Chasity, especially since she was his wife. In no way did Shana feel she was a lesbian, or even bi-sexual for that matter. In her eyes it was just a little bi-curious experience that got out of hand. *'Now Chasity is trying to fuck up everything, but I won't let it go down like that'*. First thing in the morning she decided she would change their phone number and began her search for a new apartment.

CHAPTER SIX

C-God felt it would be best to stay at a motel for a couple of days or at least until he got his head right. He figured if niggas knew where Mike was resting on the low, they more than likely knew about his spot. As Ness dropped him off, he gave him direct orders.

"Yo, go to my crib, get the yayo, the guns and here, this is the combination to the safe, bring my money too," he said handing him a small piece of paper with six digits on it.

'*Money,*' Ness thought to himself as jackpot bells went off in his head. "How much money?" He asked C-God out of curiosity.

"Shit, I don't know. It's enough though. What the fuck you worried about it for? Just bring it to me." C-God knew exactly how much money he had, but this was a test to see if he could trust Ness. "Oh and don't forget the scale, a'ight. Can you handle that? 'Cause yo, ya'll lil' niggas don't be on top of shit like my man Mike. A nigga gotta get all specific; breaking shit down for ya'll slow ass muthafuckas. So, I'm trusting you to get my shit and bring it to me. Don't fuck up! A'ight, one!" C-God said giving Ness a pound and then getting out of the hooptie. Ness quickly agreed and sped off. Wasting no time, he pulled out his cell phone and called Smitty.

"Yo, what up Smit?"

"What up nigga, how's it going down?"

"Yo man this nigga don't have a clue, he thinks it was that kid Tucker."

"Oh word, that's a good thing."

"I know, but yo, he's sending me over to his spot right now to get his shit-*all of it , yo!*"

"Yo, you for real, dawg?"

"Hell yeah nigga, I got the combination to his safe. I'm heading over there right now!"

"So yo, fuck all that other bullshit we talked about and let's get his ass now. How much shit he working with?"

"Yo, he ain't say, but that's his spot, so everything is probably up in there. I just ain't wanna straight gank his ass like that 'cause then he gon' know I did it."

"Man, fuck that punk ass muthafucka. He handing his shit right to us and with Mike gone that nigga ain't shit, dude. Besides, niggas ain't feeling him like that no more in the hood. I'm telling you, if we come around and start showing these niggas mad love, they gon' flip on that nigga C, son word up!"

Ness pulled up into a parking spot in front of C-God's building; he turned off the car and sat in silence for a moment thinking about how C had treated him like some punk ass chump. Never once did C say *'good looking out,'* or *'thanks man, you saved my fucking life.'*

"Yo, you still there," Smitty asked breaking the silence.

"Yeah."

"So what muthafucka, you need me to come hold your hand or something," laughed Smitty as he sensed some hesitation in Ness.

"Nah, dawg. I got this; I'll hit you when I'm done."

"You sure nigga 'cause I'm sensing some *nervousness* in your blood?"

"Nigga I got this, I'ma hit you back!"

"A'ight!" said Smitty.

Ness entered C-God's Hempstead apartment and greed took over instantly. Inside was 10 kilos of uncut cocaine wrapped tightly in clear plastic, about 200g's in the safe and three guns. He thought about what Smitty had said; C-God did hand every-thing to them, but he didn't expect it to be on a silver platter. All types of 'come up' schemes ran through his mind as he placed the keys in a plastic garbage bag, poured a bottle of fabric sof-tener on top to conceal the scent, and then packed it all inside a duffel bag filled with dirty clothes. There was no way Ness could take everything down to the car all at once, so he figured he'd take the drugs first and then come back for the money. The guns, he planned to leave behind. Ness entered the elevator with the duffel bag strapped across his shoulder. When the ele-vator doors opened, he headed towards the double doors, and spotted the FBI everywhere. Starting to panic, his instincts told him to run like hell, but where was he going to run to. The best thing for him to do was play it cool and proceed with the plan. Exiting the building, Ness walked past them as calm as possible. He'd been arrested enough times to know that a reaction or the slightest sign of discomfort is what they look for. Just as he had reached nearly 20 feet from the car, a voice called out to him.

"Hey boy, where you coming from?" an officer asked. Ness, shitting bricks, managed to remain calm and speak without showing any signs of nervousness.

"I'm coming from my girlfriend's house. Is there a problem Sir?"

"Well I don't know, is there? It's pretty early in the morning boy, where are you heading to? Did your girlfriend and you have a fight, 'cause that's a big ol' bag you got there."

"It's just some dirty clothes I'm taking over to the laundromat. You know, underwears, socks and tees; *would* you like to take a look Sir?" he said unzipping the bag just enough to expose the dirty clothes he had lying on top of the coke. Ness was scared shitless, but he had to take his chances hoping it would throw him off.

"No, that's okay son, by the way what did you say you your name was again," asked the officer just as he was headed back towards the building.

"It's Calvin, Calvin Greene, sir," he said smiling and lying his ass off. He knew damn well he never asked his name in the first place.

"Would you happen to know a fellow in this building that goes by the name C-God?" the officer asked.

"No officer, I don't, why? Did he do something bad, sir?" Ness pressed for info.

"Let's just say he's one of the bad guys."

"No way, officer. I stay away from them bad guys." He was really laying it on thick. "Far away! I'm a good guy, you know I have a nine to five. As a matter of fact, I was just promoted to supervisor at my job."

"Really and where is that?" asked the officer.

"Mac Donald's, and one day I hope to open a franchise of my own." Ness couldn't believe the bullshit coming from his own mouth.

"Alright kid, good for you, just stay out of trouble." The officer said heading towards the building as he spotted the K-9 unit pulling up.

'Oh shit,' Ness thought as he opened his car door in a hurry, jumped in and pulled off immediately before the dogs caught a whiff of what was really in the bag. Sweating bullets, he knew how close he came to getting knocked. He started to laugh thinking about how well he played that pig.

"Ahhh Fuck!" Ness yelled , remembering what he left behind. "Damn, why I ain't take the fucking money." Pulling his cell phone from his pocket he dialed C's cell. C-God saw Ness's number come up on the phone and picked up beefing.

"You's a stupid muthafucka, why the fuck is you calling me from your cell nigga?"

"Yo C, I know but -"

"No nigga, obviously you don't know! Go find a fucking payphone and - nah you know what, fuck all that, just bring my shit to me," he said with such authority in his disrespectful tone before hanging up.

"Fuck you nigga! You ain't got your shit," Ness yelled as he threw his phone in the passenger's seat. "I ain't giving that nigga shit." He had a plan and C-God was going to no choice but to step down for Ness' takeover, or die. His plan was simple—set up shop with the bricks and flip the profit. It would take some careful planning but Ness had the overall scheme ready. He did-n't really know much about pushing weight, but Smitty did. Now all he needed was a few soldiers behind him, just in case C-God tried to get at him. Ness remembered the wild stories from back in the days about the fear C-God pumped into nigga's hearts. But, for the past few years he'd been rolling with him all he wit-nessed was his sharp ass tongue. It was Mike who always pulled the trigger for him and he's been dismissed. *'So what next?'* Ness thought. After watching C-God get weak over a broad, Ness no longer respected his gangsta. Of course he wasn't gon' straight sleep on the nigga neither because it was always better to be safe then sorry. Establishing a squad that was ready for war was first on his list of things to do, you know, just to be on the safe side of the fence. Ness stopped at a pay phone and called C back.

"Yo, who this?" C answered his cell on the third ring.

"Yo man, it's Ness. Listen I ain't got your shit dawg. I went to the crib and the Feds was all over place. They had dogs and all types of shit. So a nigga just kept going."

"Yo what the fuck, did they get in my crib?" C-God asked.

"They was running up in the building, I ain't even get out the car. All I seen was police rolling deep and I got the fuck up out the area."

"So yo, wait a little while, go scoop up Reg, then go back over there and check that shit out. It might not even be my spot they hit." C- God ordered.

"Nah, dawg. I ain't going back over there." Ness said.

"What the fuck you mean you ain't going back over there?"

"Yo son, check this out if they ran up in your shit, then nine times out of ten they still there, or they watching it and I ain't getting caught up in that, dawg," Ness said standing his ground and refusing to let C-God punk him.

"Yo, you bitch ass nigga, what the fuc-" Before C-God could finish his verbal lashing, the payphone operator asked for five more cents for the next two minutes and Ness hung up.

He got back in his hooptie and fumble through the arm rest for some sounds, music was always his motivation. He was excited about his chance to finally make some real doe. Finding a tape he popped it in and turned up the volume.

'First you get the money, then you get the power, after the power then these muthafuckas will respect you.'

Ness had one more important phone call to make.

"Yo, we on nigga. We working with ten of them things nigga and shit look sweet too!" Ness didn't need to go into details, his partner knew exactly how it was going down.

"That's what's up! So yo, let's get up in a little while and get this shit popping, a'ight?" said Smitty.

"Sounds like a plan." Ness responded as they abided by one of the most important rules in the drug game—*watch what you say over the phone and keep it short.*

CHAPTER SEVEN

It was shortly after seven am when Mrs. Wright got over the initial shock of someone trying to murder her daughter. She didn't feel up to it, but she knew it was necessary to call the family and Epiphany's closest friends. Of course as far as friends go, Keisha was #1, then came Shana, who she was unable to reach. When Mrs. Wright broke the news to Keisha, she was devastated. After some encouraging words about Epiphany's condition and the doctor's reassurance that she would pull through this; Keisha managed to calm down long enough to get the details on what they believed happened. Mrs. Wright questioned her about the guy who was murdered while visiting Epiphany, but she couldn't remember his name and Keisha couldn't offer much help.

"Keisha you are the closest friend Epiphany has, you two are like sisters. I am her mother, so she tells me nothing and if I do hear anything, I hear it from the streets. I know she talks to you. So I need to ask you something and I want you to be straight with me, okay?" she asked Keisha in all seriousness.

"Okay, I'll do my best." Keisha replied in a soft voice.

"Was she still messing around with that Hinderson boy?"

"Mrs. Wright, in all honesty I don't know. I wanna say no 'cause the last time we talked about him she told me it was over. She found out about some girl he had gotten pregnant and supposedly she ended it with him."

"Keisha, I just have one more question. Do you think he had something to do with this?" She asked as tears formed and her voice started to crack.

"Mrs. Wright, you know C-god stepped to Tucker over some nonsense a while ago. He's made threats and as a matter of fact he's the reason why Tucker doesn't feel it's safe to stay at home with me and the baby. So, to answer your question, yes I do think he had something to do with this. I don't like him, nor do I trust him and I strongly believe he's absolutely capable of doing something like this." Keisha was starting to get angry.

"Even though she was pregnant?" Mrs. Wright questioned in disbelief. *How he could he be so cold-hearted*, she wondered.

"Wait a minute, Epiphany is pregnant?" Keisha couldn't believe her ears.

"She *was*." Mrs. Wright said sadly.

"That bastard! How could he? Mrs. Wright, I gotta go. I have to call Tucker, but I'll be at the hospital as soon as I reach him, okay?" Keisha's eyes flooded with tears all over again.

Keisha arrived at the hospital alone. Carrying 'get well soon' balloons and some flowers, she had only a half an hour left before morning visiting hours were over. Seeing Epiphany was something she had to do, but her mind couldn't stop wondering about Tucker. He'd been ignoring her calls all morning. *'He really might not forgive me'* she thought. Regardless of the circumstances, she felt she was still the mother of his child and there was no excuse for his behavior. She ran into Epiphany's dad, who was standing at the elevator when she got off. Jay Wright looked like an exhausted mad man. He showed her to the room and thanked her for coming, before heading out. As Keisha entered the room she felt sick. She hated the smell of hospitals— to her they represented sickness and death.

Epiphany's mom greeted her with a tight hug.

"Where is Tucker?" Keisha's heart dropped into the pit of her stomach. She didn't have an answer, so she thought up a quick lie.

"Loretta and my sisters weren't able to make it back in time to watch the baby, so he stayed home with him," she said looking down at the floor.

"Oh, okay. How is that handsome little boy of yours?" Epiphany's mom smiled but her eyes were still puffy and her voice was rather hoarse from her lack of sleep and crying she'd been doing all night. Mrs. Wright was trying to make light of the situation, but Keisha knew she was having a hard time dealing with everything. Epiphany was her pride and joy even though she didn't always approve of the life she was living.

"He's doing great." Keisha answered back.

"Good! Well I'll give you a little time alone with Epee. I'll be back shortly, okay sweetie?"

"Okay!" Keisha walked closer to Epiphany's bedside. Seeing Epiphany lying there like that brought Keisha to tears. Her face was bruised up pretty badly. She pulled up a chair and moved in as close as she could to the side of the bed. Taking Epiphany's hand into hers, she began to talk to her.

"Hey E, it's me Keisha. I know your in bad shape right now, but your gonna pull through this. I know you will because you know the world can't make it without Epiphany J. Wright." She let out a little laugh. "We just can't do it without you girl. So, you better hurry up and get better before I go crazy. You're my best friend and I love you, plus I need you to help me fix this mess with Tucker. I'm in the dog house and he'll probably never take me back, let alone trust me. I should have never let Lea talk me into having strippers at my bachelorette party. I know it's nobody's fault that I fucked Damager, but if his ass wasn't there in the first place—doing all them freaky things to me, while I was drunk—none of this would have happened. And that damn tape-", she drifted off into a distasteful thought.

"Anyway I won't get into that right now." Keisha quickly snapping out of her daydream and changed the subject.

"Girl your godson is getting so big. He's trying to walk now and he's got eight teeth—ain't that something? He's a real cutie though. I know all mothers think they're kids are cute, but my son is just gorgeous and I' m not just saying that cause he's mines neither. Seriously girl," she laughed, "you know what I was thinking about on the ride over here? I was thinking about the times when we use to just wild out? What were we, like, fourteen then? Yeah 'cause that was before I started going out with Tucker.

Girl we use to have so much fun together back then. Remember the time we got kicked out of that club? That was so funny. We beat a nigga down for touching you on your ass remember? And, he had the audacity to stand there and pop shit about doing it too. You was so mad, you just turned around and snuffed his ass. Then of course me and Shana looked at each other and then followed your lead. We jumped on him and commenced to whipping his ass. Boy, nobody could tell us nothing that night. We thought we was the shit for fucking him up the way we did. That was so funny" Keisha laughed again as she continued her one-sided conversation down memory lane. "Oh…oh. remember the time we cut school and took the J train all the way to *west bubble fuck* Brooklyn? Playing hooky with those derelicts we met in the pizza shop on the Ave. They were some frontin' ass niggas, but cute as hell though. The one you was kicking with was the cutest, damn he was fine. Did you fuck him? 'Cause ya'll was locked in the room for a long time. I know you probably did 'cause he was gorgeous. He had those pretty green eyes and that good hair, all curly and whatnot. You use to be soft on them pretty boys back then. And Kobe. Yuck! I'll never forget his name. That was the one I hooked up with. He wasn't bad looking neither, but ole boy's breath was kicking. I kept trying to offer him some gum and he would not take it. Oh my god, his mouth smelled like it took a shit. I was so glad he didn't try to kiss me or anything.

Those niggas really tried to get grimey on us once Shana got into it with the guy she was hooked up with. Remember that? He wanted some ass and she fronted. Was he thirsty, or what?

Wanting to fight her over some pussy, remember? He pulled out that knife and kicked us all out. I couldn't believe he kicked us out, knowing they said they was gonna send us back home in a cab if we came over. They tried to play us for real. But it was all good though, 'cause your sneaky ass was always ahead of the game. You copped that pretty boy's chain and his little corny ass nugget bracelet without him even knowing it. We hopped our ass back on the J train to Jamaica with the quickness, went to the Coliseum, traded that nigga's jewels in and got us each a pair of bamboo earrings. That was crazy. You was scandalous girl. We always had each other's back.

I tried calling Shana but her phone has been disconnected. Her cell ain't working either. It's like she ain't part of the crew no more. We're all moving in different directions, but when I leave here, I think I'm just gonna stop by her house to see what's up with her." Keisha could have went on and on, reminiscing about the good ol'times, but the announcements came on saying that visiting hours were now over.

"I gotta go now, but I'll be back tomorrow" Keisha said as she kissed Epiphany on the forehead and headed towards the door.

"Keisha wait," Mrs. Wright called out as she spotted her walking down the hallway. Keisha stopped and turned around.

"I just wanted to thank you once again for coming and remind you to tell Tucker to please keep his ears open in the streets. Oh, and remember I was telling you about the guy they found dead at Epee's apartment? You knew him, I found out that he was one of her old boyfriends. His name was...something like, Mahkai."

"Oh no, Mrs. Wright, please tell me you don't mean Malikai?"

"Yeah that's him. Wasn't he a friend of Tucker's?"

"Oh god, I gotta go." Keisha barley made it out the hospital before she dialed Tucker cell. Again, she got no answer, so she

33

waited for the beep. "Why aren't you picking up your cell-phone?" she screamed into the receiver. "Mali is dead and Epiphany is lying up in the fucking hospital. Damn T, I know you hate me right now but they're our friends. Please call me back." Keisha hung up.

Seconds later, her cell rang. Keisha answered before the first rang even finished and cried out Tucker's name. Only the voice on the other end wasn't him, it was Julius aka *'The Damager'*. Her crying kind of threw him off, he paused for a moment before he spoke.

"Ahhh…is this Keisha?" he asked hesitantly.

"Who is this?" she cried.

"It's Julius, are you alright?"

"No, I'm not alright and please don't call me anymore" Keisha screamed, taking her anger out on him and abruptly ending his call. She dialed Tucker again, expecting the voicemail, but was thrown off when he answered.

"What, Keish?" Tucker was short with her.

"H… he-l-l-o," she stuttered into the mouth piece of the phone.

"Yeah, what?" He replied.

"Did you get my message?" Keisha asked nervously.

"Which one?"

"The one I just left about Malikai and Epiphany."

"Nah, but Momma D already told me about Mali. She's fucked up over this shit. I just came from identifying his body and I'm just as fucked up. Everything is fucked up. I gotta bury my best friend. I gotta take care of his funeral arrangements. Damn! I can't believe this shit." For a moment there was complete silence. "What's up with Epiphany though?"

Keisha could hear the sadness in Tuckers' voice although he was trying hard to act like everything was under control. She knew he was going through hell right now. She added her deepest regards first before telling him about the condition Epiphany was in.

"Hmmm, so she gon' be a'ight, right?"

"Well, the doctors are hopeful. You know she was pregnant?"

"By who? That nigga C?" He said answering his own question.

"I don't know."

"She probably had Mali set up. She told that nigga C-God that Mali was going to be there." Tucker jumped to conclusions about what he thought happened that night.

"Oh, come on Tucker. That's ridiculous and if that was the case, why is she lying up in the ICU?"

"Maybe the nigga was just using her, got what he wanted, then tried to kill two birds with one stone. Or maybe, she was shot as part of the plan to look innocent. Who knows?"

"What! Epiphany would never do something like that" said Keisha speaking in her friend's defense. "Besides she really cared about Malikai."

"Cared! "What's that suppose to mean? You supposedly *loved* me, but that ain't stop you from getting it on with the next nigga, did it? "I ain't putting nothing past a bitch no more" Keisha realized that Tucker was no longer talking about Epiphany and Mali. He was talking about her.

"BITCH! You know what, I'ma let that go because you just lost your best friend. Yes I played myself, but you better not ever fix your face to call me out my name again. I am your son's mother, just in case you forgot and regardless of what you might think of me right now, that part won't ever change. So, while you try your best to make me feel worst then I already do, you need to ask yourself why I did what I did, *Mr. Get-money-and-never–have-time-for-anything-else.*" Keisha said sarcastically.

"Yeah, getting money for what though, Keisha? Could it be that six-hundred thousand dollar house we living in and the expensive ass cars we got? Is that the money you talking about, it gotta be?"

"No, I'm talking about the money that keeps you out of town all time, my needs neglected and your black ass in troub-"

"Yeah the money that I was out there busting my ass for just to keep shit comfortable for us, while you go out and get fucked, RIGHT!" Keisha didn't say a word. How could she? He *was* right.

"Yeah, yeah, yeah I didn't think you wanted to go there. Where's my son at anyway?"

"He's home."

"Well listen, after the funeral, I want you, your Moms, the baby and your sisters to go on vacation or something. At least until shit blows over. Go back to Atlanta with them if you want. Your family came all the way up here for a wedding and since you fucked that up maybe you should just take them somewhere. Miami, Mexico or even Disneyland - wherever. I don't care, just go somewhere until things calm down a bit. And Keisha, I ain't asking you, I'm telling you. I already lost my boy and I ain't trying to take no more losses, so make it happen a'ight? I gotta go." Tucker abruptly ended the call.

"Tucker, hello?" Keisha repeated his name hoping he was still on the line, but there was nothing but silence. She was pissed off, but at this point she didn't feel the need to call him back just to argue. Keisha knew exactly what he was going through 'cause she was going through it too. But, because of her mistakes they couldn't be there for each other.

CHAPTER EIGHT

Shana arrived home late in the afternoon, exhausted and in a not so pleasant mood. Not only did she lose sleep worrying about Chasity's craziness and Smitty's motives, but she was up and out early searching for a new place. Out of the six apartments she viewed that day not one of them was to her liking. To make matters worst, when she opened the door to her small basement apartment there were no 'hello', 'how you doing?', or 'how's your day?', but instead beefing.

"Yo, how the fuck you gonna go change numbers without telling a nigga? I got muthafuckas calling me for some important shit and they can't even get in touch with me 'cause your stupid ass done went and changed the number. Then I tried to get in touch with you on your cell and you done change that, too. And why you had the ringer turned off on the phone, Shana? Huh? What the fuck is up with that? I told your sneaky ass to tie up all them loose ends with whatever crab ass niggas you was fucking with before I came the fuck home. Smitty said he tried calling me 'bout four times last night and the phone just rang and rang. Shit you even heard me tell the nigga to call and you still went and did some stupid shit like that." Shana wasn't in the mood to argue, which was rare because normally she would have been all up in K.C. shit. She never backed down from an argument with him, even when it got physical. K.C. lived for drama, so he made it hard for Shana to ignore him. He would go on and on until he got a response. And that's exactly what he got. Shana listened quietly to him bitch, while he sat on her couch, playing her play station, about changing her number to her phones until her head felt like it was going to explode.

"Shut the fuck up nigga. So what I changed the numbers, they're *my* fucking numbers anyway. You only been home what, *a day and a half* and already you starting to get on a bitch nerves," she yelled.

"Oh, why am I getting on ya nerves? 'Cause a nigga fucked up, huh? Fresh out the joint and I ain't got shit. Now, all of a sudden I'm getting on your nerves? That's what it is, huh? But when a nigga was getting paper, it was a whole other story, right Sha?" K.C. paused the game and walked over to Shana. "I remember when my shit was all good, you wouldn't let a nigga breath then. Now you wanna come at me with *my* phone, *my* this and *my* that. You got it twisted, for real. Just 'cause you laid a few dollars on a nigga's books and bought a few funky ass outfits for me to come home in, don't mean shit. You need to stop tripping the fuck out. Acting like you forgot some of the shit I did for you. I see how a bitch change up when she think a nigga need her muthafucking ass though, but I'm a be back on soon, real soon," said K.C., his face was now less than an inch from her's.

"Yeah, well I see how quick a nigga can change up from all that sweet shit you was kicking when you was locked the fuck up. So what, you don't need a bitch no more 'cause you free?" Shana said taking a step back.

"Yo Sha, just shut up!" K.C. turned around, sat back on the couch and reach for the remote.

"Whatever." Shana went into the bedroom, closing the door behind her. The argument was over but her headache was just beginning.

"Yo Sha you still ain't give me the number." K.C yelled out loud enough for her to hear from behind the closed door.

Shana had left the new numbers big and bold on the refrigerator for K.C. to spot before she left this morning. She figured he would notice it at some point during the day, but obviously not. Avoiding any further conflict she wrote both numbers down on a piece of paper, opened the bedroom door, handed it to him, walked back to the room and shut the door. She woke up about two hours later to find K.C. in the same spot still playing video games. On her way to the kitchen, K.C. told her the horrible news.

"Yo, Sha" he said "What's that broad's name, you use to run around with all the time? Shana, started to get a little nervous, afraid he might of heard something about Chasity.

"What broad K.C?" She replied snobbishly.

"You know? That stuck up light-skinned bitch with the long hair."

"Oh, Epiphany!" Shana said as her nerves begun to settle down.

"Yeah, her."

"What about her?"

"I heard niggas ran up in her crib and let off some lead in that ass, that's what!"

"And who told you that?" Shana almost dropped her glass of juice.

"Yo, that's your friend right?" K.C. sarcastically asked.

"Yeah." Shana responded with a sarcastic look on her face.

"A'ight then, don't worry about who told me. Just be glad they did." K.C. arrogantly replied. Shana rushed back to the bedroom to call Keisha and find out if it was true, because she would be the first to hear anything about Epiphany.

"Hello?" Keisha sounded like she was sleeping."

"Hey Keish, it's me Shana."

"I know, I've been trying to get in touch with you. Epiphany's in the hospital, she got shot."

"I just heard that? Is she alright? What happened?" Even thought they had their share of differences, Shana still cared for Epiphany more then she showed.

"I don't really know exactly what happened, but whoever's responsible killed Malikai too," Keisha said.

"Wait a minute, Malikai is dead?" Shana was in shock.

"Yeah. And my guess is that, that black motherfucker, C-God, had something to do with it" Keisha fumed.

"You think he would - never mind." Shana put some thought into who they were talking about. She knew damn well C-God was capable of a stunt like this. "So how's Epiphany doing?" she asked.

"She's alive, but hooked up to all kinds of tubes. I went to see her today and seeing her lying there like broke my heart. That bastard really did my girl dirty." Keisha began to sob. "Well is she gon' be a'ight?"

"The doctors said she will," Keisha whispered.

"Damn, I know Tucker must be taking Malikai's murder hard."

"Girl, hard ain't the word. There's so much other shit going on right now. It's crazy." Keisha felt so distant from Shana, so she wasn't going to tell her everything.

"When are you going to visit Epiphany again?"

"Everyday until she comes home. Why?"

"Because, I wanna go with you tomorrow," Shana answered.

"That's cool. I'll call you in the morning."

"Yeah, but wait, first let me give you my new numbers," Shana said.

CHAPTER NINE

Shana and Keisha had been spending a lot of time together. Mainly back and forth to the hospital visiting Epiphany, which that gave them a lot of time to talk. Keisha finally poured out her guts to Shana about the tape, the canceling of the wedding and the drama with Tucker. Shana was vexed that one of those jealous bitches at the party could play Keisha like that. She wanted to help Keisha find out who was responsible.

The two of them arrived at Malikai's funeral a little early. It was Keisha's idea. She hoped to see Tucker and maybe get a moment of his time; not to bring up their situation, but to be an extra shoulder if he needed it. Of course it didn't work out that way. Tucker took one look at her, turned up his face and walked right past her. Shana noticed his look of disgust.

"Keisha maybe now is not the best time to approach him," she advised.

"It might not be, but I have too." Keisha was really desperate.

"You sure, 'cause I ain't never seen him look at you like that before, Keisha."

"That's because you haven't seen him lately. What's the worst that could happen? He's not gonna make a scene and embarrass me, not here anyway."

"A'ight Keish, but if he does, I got your back."

"He won't," Keisha said as she slowly walked over to Tucker. This was the first time in a long she'd seen him in a suit and although he hated her guts she wanted nothing more but to tell him how good he looked and make sweet love to him.

"Hey T, how you holding up?" Tucker slightly rolled his eyes and shook his head.

"I'm good, where's my son at?" He asked.

"Is that all you got to say to me? 'Where's my son at?'"

"Yep." Tucker said coldly.

"Well he's at home with my mother."

"Did you make those arrangements we talked about?"

"What arrangements?"

"Keisha, I told you to book a flight somewhere for you and your family until shit calms down a bit. What, you forgot?" Tucker forgetting where he was, began to raise his voice.

"Oh, yeah I did that already. I just had to pay my last respects to Mali before we left." Keisha was lying, but she knew that's what Tucker wanted to hear. She did plan on getting around to it.

"Good," Tucker said, turning to walk away. People started to arrive and the self-appointed host, had to go shake hands.

"T, do you plan on talking to me before I leave?" Keisha grabbed his arm and spoke softly.

"About what, Keish? There ain't really nothing to talk about?" Tucker lowered his voice, so the guest couldn't hear him.

"Tucker, I'm sorry. I was so drunk, I didn't mean to do it, please just -"

"Look Keisha, not now." Tucker took her by the hand and pulled her into the hallway. "I don't know if I'll ever be ready to talk about it. You can cry and say your sorry until you turn blue in the face, but it don't mean nothing to me. Keisha, you should of thought about all that before you let dude run up in my pussy. You fucked up, but I just hope it was worth it." His voice started to crack. Tucker walked away, leaving Keisha right were she stood. Shana rushed over to comfort her.

"Come on Keish, stop crying. If he wants to act like that then fuck him. You tried."

Keisha couldn't stop crying though, the thought of Tucker not wanting her any more pained her so bad. She loved him so much, but the way he was acting towards her made her question his love for her. He could've at least heard her out. Yeah she fucked up really bad and no it wasn't worth it, but she was truly sorry.

"Come on Keisha, the service is about to start." Shana put her arms around Keisha and walked her over to the seats she was holding for them.

Flowers were everywhere and on both ends of the platinum-colored casket stood bleeding hearts made out of fresh red and white roses. Tucker took care of all the arrangements. People came out of the woodworks to say their final goodbyes and of course a few haters pop in as well. *'It's just sad that it takes a death to bring so many people together,'* Tucker thought as he stood near Pee and Corn, who acted as armed security at the door, just in case niggas wanted to act up. Tucker personally greeted most of the mourners that entered the funeral home. A couple of them even pulled him to the side to share different versions of hearsay from the streets about what happened.

Pictures of Mali were all over the place. Due to his disfigurement the casket was closed and Tucker preferred it that way. He wanted today to be more of an remembrance rather than a farewell. He wanted the pictures of Malikai to remind people of the life he lived, the fun he had and what a loving person he was. Momma D was the only one allowed a final viewing of her only son before the service started. She managed to keep her composure during the viewing and service, but she broke down at the burial.

"It's so Hard to Say Goodbye to Yesterday" played softly as loved ones and friends dropped red roses onto Malikai's casket as it was being lowered into the ground. Tucker stayed by Momma D's side the whole time. While trying his best to stay strong for her, he was torn apart on the inside and needed Momma D to lean on just as much as she needed him.

CHAPTER TEN

C-God was furious. He found out that Ness had betrayed him. The Feds did run up in his spot, but no drugs were reportedly found and only 50g's out of two-hundred thousand, a scale and a few minor items were confiscated. Also, word on the street was that Ness was the one responsible for Mikes' murder and now was running around acting like Bishop (Tupac's character in the movie *Juice*). C-God tried for days to get at his workers, but none of them returned his calls. Finally he got in touch with Reggie, one of his regular runners.

"Yo Reg, what up with ya'll niggas, don't nobody answer their cell phones no more? Just 'cause a nigga go on a hiatus for a week or so, to get his head right; nigga's fall off track and forget what's good?" C-God said.

"Yo C man, niggas ain't running with you no more. They done got down with that kid Ness. He be showing us mad love in the hood, making sure we all eat."

"Oh, so you down with the nigga too?" C-God asked as he sniffed a long line of cocaine from the glass plate in front of him.

"Yo, I'm saying, dude do look out and you know what I'm up against. I just wanted to give you a heads up man, 'cause shit is real out here," Reg said. C-God was outraged, he jumped up and smashed the glass plate.

"You muthafuckas think I'm gonna sit back and eat shit. I'll kill all ya'll niggas. Ya'll ma'fuckers gon' do me like this, turn around and betray me—the hand that fed ya'll niggas for years. YA'LL SOME DEAD MUTHA'FUCKAS, YA HEARD!!! FUCKING DEAD!!!!!" Just as C-God was about to hang up, Ness walked over and snatched the phone from Reg.

"Yo, is that that bitch ass nigga C?" He questioned. Reggie shook his head yes and Ness put the phone to his ear.

"Yo man save all that bullshit you talking nigga. If your heart was as big as that fucking mouth of yours, your punk ass might not be in this situation, now would you, huh nigga? You soft dukes. I should of let that ho kill your bitch ass. It's over for you now, son. You had your turn now I'm running this. See, I'm being a nice guy about it, letting your punk ass live. I know Mike wished I was nice enough to let him and his family live, but it bee's like that sometimes." Ness laughed. "So yo, man to bitch, I suggest you break out; go hide up under a rock or something. 'Cause ya nobody dawg, ya nobody 'til somebody splits that fucking wig of yours. So bring your bitch ass back around, thinking shit's sweet, and I promise you *I'm a make you famous.* One!"

Talking greasy to C-God like that got Ness's adrenaline pumping. He was hyped and ready for whatever came his way. C-God was fuming. Normally he'd call Mike to kill a nigga that crossed him the way Ness did, but Mike was gone. Everyone on his team was gone. There was nothing else for him to do but get skidded. Locked up in his hotel room, C-God sniffed so much coke his noise started to bleed. He only had access to about five grand and that was gonna have to hold him down until he came up with a plan. He knew it would be hard to go up against those niggas as a one-man band. Another problem was the Feds; they were hot on his trail, so C-God decided the best thing for him to do was skip town and lay low for awhile. Team or no team, they hadn't heard the last from Corey Hinderson.

CHAPTER 11

As she walked down what appeared to be a very long tunnel, Epiphany heard a voice calling her name. It was coming from behind her, the voice was male and sounded familiar. Afraid, she paused for a moment as the voice continued to call out to her. It was as if they were in some sort of danger. Epiphany hesitantly turned around, something inside of her forced her to follow the voice. As she followed the voice she could see a beaming ray of light and the further she walked the brighter the light got. The light was her guide. Suddenly she could see images of her life posted up on the tunnel's walls. The good, the bad, and the ugly had all been caught on film. She felt like she was trapped in a projection room that featured "The Life and Times of Epiphany Janee Wright." There were moments she spent as a child with her parents, moments with friends and even x-rated moments she shared with many men including her uncle, who molested her. *This is some weird shit,* Epiphany thought , but yet by her being so vain she found this experience to be fascinating—watching her life, her memories, and her personal moments. All of it, from adolescence to adulthood surrounded her. Either this was her journey to heaven, or hell. The weighing of her good deeds and her sins.

As she continued down the long tunnel, the sound of her name became louder. When she finally reached the end she saw Malikai smiling at her. He was dressed in an all white suit, with a pimp daddy hat slightly cocked to the side and looked heaven sent to her. He had been calling out to her all along. Once she approached him no words were exchanged and although he was smiling, she could still see that there was some sadness in his eyes. He wrapped his arms around her tightly as if he would never see her again. His body temperature was so cold. Epiphany tried to speak to him, but her words could not escape her mouth. She felt numb. Suddenly, darkness filled the hall. Everything had faded right before her eyes, Malikai, the images and the light. Epiphany stood alone at the end of the tunnel. Malikai had just saved her from eternal darkness and it was time for her to go home.

Epiphany's Mom noticed slight movement from Epiphany for the first time. Her eyelids were shut but her eyeballs moved as if she was trying to open them.

"It's been two weeks, wake up out of that misery, Epee," her mom whispered as she reached for her daughter's hand. "I know you're a fighter, your father knows you're a fighter, your friends know and even these doctor know. So fight baby, make your way back. You're too strong to be lying up in this damn hospital bed like this. Do you hear me?" Epiphany didn't respond with words, but she squeezed her mothers hand just enough to let her know she heard her. That was all the assurance Mrs. Wright needed. She knew Epiphany would pull through for sure now. She walked over towards the window and dialed her husband immediately to share the news, but wasn't able to reach him. Mrs. Wright just stared out of the window, wondering where her husband could be that he wasn't answering his phone.

Jay Wright had been on a mission since the incident happened. He felt he owed it to his babygirl to find the bastards responsible and see to it that they suffered the same way his family had. He didn't give a fuck about the police; they had yet to be of any help. Besides, he felt jail would be too easy for the punk. Mrs. Wright definitely wanted whoever was to blame to suffer as well, but just not at the hands of her husband. She had waited a long time for Jay to give up that gangsta shit and there was no way she was going back to living that kind of lifestyle with him. Epiphany had been lying in a coma for two weeks, but to her it seemed more like months or years and every day was a struggle. Mrs. Wright looked towards the Lord to pull her through. She always believed in him; although she never appreciated how good he'd been to her and her family over the years. It took a tragedy to open her eyes and make her realize that she had a lot to be grateful for. Jay was in the drug game for over twenty-five years and somehow he never been locked up, shot, robbed, or killed. Harm had never crossed the Wright's path, nor have they ever hit any financial hardships. *That had to have been the work of the Lord*, she thought. So she was finally ready to give thanks and praise him. *God only knows, It's long overdue, but never too late.* Tiara Wright joined the Born Again Baptist Community Church and the changes within her had been miraculous.

"Mommy," Epiphany said, strangely looked around the hospital room. Mrs. Wright froze in disbelief, that word sounded like a sweet melody, music to her ears.

"Praise the Lord, thank you Jesus," Mrs. Wright closed her eyes and said a little prayer before rushing to Epiphany's bedside.

Right away Epiphany started to panic as she continued to look around at her unfamiliar surroundings. She began to forcefully pull at the IV tubes in her arm and question about her whereabouts over and over again. Her mom tried her best to calm her down, but decided it would be best to call in the nurse. Two nurses rushed in and immediately tried to relax Epiphany, but she continued to struggle. One of the nurses, a heavy-set older woman, used her weight to restrain Epiphany long enough for the other nurse to inject her with a sedative. She explained to Epiphany's mom that the sedative was a mild one, just enough to help Epiphany relax a bit. She also explained that it was likely for a patient to react this way when awakening from a coma with no recollection of what happened to them. The medication worked instantly, Epiphany began to settle down. Mrs. Wright reached for her cellphone and called Jay again. This time he answered.

"Hello?"

"Baby, where were you? Didn't I tell you? I told you she was gon' pull through." Mrs. Wright couldn't control her excitement.

"Epee's awake?" asked Jay.

"Yes honey, she woke up swinging."

"Get the fuck out of here, baby are you serious?" Finally Jay started to believe his wife. He was cheesing from ear to ear.

"Yes, wait baby, hold on for a minute." Tiara placed her cell to Epiphany's ear.

Epiphany softly mumbled, "Hello?"

There was nothing more to say, Jay Wright was on his way.

CHAPTER 12

The Feds had all operations shut down for a minute. They ran up in every spot possibly linked to C-God. They offered 'get out of jail free' cards and all kind of plea bargains to the small time hustlers that got caught up in the sweeps if in return they could give up any helpful information that could lead them straight to C-God or linked him to Malikai's murder. The Feds wanted C-God and niggas were ready to snitch him out, but no one knew his whereabouts. C-God never really showed his workers no love on the streets, so they ain't have none for him. While he was driving his tricked out Cadillac Escalade, peeling off hundreds for bottles at the clubs, flossing, his workers were barely getting by. After making the minimum—enough doe for an outfit, but not enough for the footwear, or vice versa—for so long, a niggas was ready for him to fall. The heat was coming from all angles. C-God had the Feds after his freedom, a mob of niggas trying to take his life plus Ness and Smitty taking over his business.

Peewee and Cornell made a trip to New York to personally do C-God some harm. They ran up in his parent's home, guns exposed and scared Mrs. Hinderson so bad she suffered a massive heart attack and died on the spot. Poppa Hinderson watched helplessly right before Peewee shot him in his head. On their way out of C-gods parents house, Peewee and Cornell joked about how easy a job it was. Since Tucker left strict orders to leave C-God's kids out of their beef, the two knew that the death of his parents would definitely get a rise out of him. They assumed that aside from his kids, his folks were probably the only other people he held dear because everybody knew he treated all his baby mommas like shit. He ain't give a fuck about none of them and two of them was smoked out on crack, so getting rid of those bitches wouldn't phase C-god. It would've been a favor to him and it made no since to waste the lead. Tucker knew the deaths of C's parents would get him to surface sooner or later, but for right now it was best for him to lay low and just wait. Peewee and Cornell headed back to the Dirty South until further notice. Once they got home, they established their business 'cause with the start-up tools Tucker gave them. It was on and popping. Tucker hit them off with five keys and put them on to his Columbian connect as a token of his appreciation for their latest endeavor. Peewee and Cornell were about to get it crunk down in the Carolinas.

CHAPTER 13

"Finally something good happened." A smile spread across Keisha's face when she received the news from Mrs. Wright that Epiphany had regained consciousness that night. Morning couldn't have come fast enough for Keisha who wanted to rush to her best friend's side. She also couldn't wait to hear Epiphany's details on what happened and who was responsible. Keisha had been spending so much of her time at the hospital that she almost forgot that her own life was still in shambles. Keisha became very depressed by all the bad that had been surrounding her life lately and wondered how she was gonna weather this terrible storm. On several occasions she tried to see Tucker, so they could sit down and discuss her affair and their future, but he was avoiding her. Sure he'd call, but only to ask about his son. Keisha didn't push the issue because she was the one that fucked things up between them. Tucker did his best to remind her that she was to blame every chance he got. At the same time she needed to understand what was going on with him. Could they work it out or should she do the unthinkable and just let him go.

'*Maybe he's just not ready to forgive me, but he will. He's just playing hardball, acting like he could careless about us,*' she tried to rationalize the reason for his behavior. Sometimes he was almost convincing, but Keisha knew better. Deep down past the hurt she knew he still loved her. That was her motivation to keep trying. She even decided to take his advice—well part of it anyway—by sending Loretta and her sisters on a real vacation to wherever her budget could afford. Unfortunately her mom declined because the girls' spring break from school was just about over and she had no more vacation time at work, so they were headed back to Atlanta soon. Loretta could sense that her daughter needed her to stay around a little longer to help out with the baby; however she also knew that her daughter's pride would never allow her to come out and say it.

"Look Keisha, I know your up under a lot of stress right now. So why don't I take the baby back with me, just for a couple of weeks, to give you and Tucker a little time to try and work things out a bit. And Nana would love to see her great-grandson," said Loretta.

"Umm" Keisha hesitated. *'What kind of mom would I be if I just shipped my son off with her?'* she thought. Loretta noticed her daughter's uneasiness and spoke in her own defense.

"Listen Keisha, I'm not the same person I was when you were growing up. I was a drunk who cared about nothing but getting drunk, but I've changed my life around completely, not just for the moment. I love my grandchild as much as I love you and your sisters and I want to be a part of his life. I can't change the past honey, but at least let me be here for you now. If you don't want him to go than that's fine with me. As long as it's not because you feel he won't be in good hands, okay sweetie?" The resentment Keisha still had towards her mom did pop into her head. She thought back to her childhood when Loretta would get drunk, pass out and sleep for days without moving. Keisha would get so hysterical thinking that her mother was dead. The 'new' Loretta had already proved she'd changed. She was such a big help with the baby. Especially since the whole fall out with Tucker. Keisha had been having a hard time trying to deal with the stress and take care of her son and her responsibilities at the same time. Half the time when she was home, she'd lock herself in her bedroom. *'I know I haven't been the best Mommy lately. What will Tucker say if I let the baby go without me? It doesn't sound like a bad idea after all,'* she thought. So much was going on at once she didn't even have the time to get down to the bottom of the whole sex tape mystery, but please believe she didn't forgot. Keisha was going to get her life back in order. With all that in mind she agreed to let Lil' T go to Atlanta, but only for a couple of weeks. Keisha also let Loretta know how much she appreciated all that she was doing.

"You don't have to thank me because you already have," Loretta smiled, "just by allowing me into you and my grandson's life." Tears ran down both of their faces as they embraced each other. Soon everything was a go. The flights were booked and in two days Keisha would have the house to herself and her plans would be set.

CHAPTER 14

"Hey, Daddy," Epiphany said as she opened her eyes. It was the second day she'd been awake.

"Hey baby girl," J Wright answered back as he leaned over and planted a kiss on her forehead. "You had me scared for a minute, Epee."

"I did? What happened to me, how did I end up here?" Epiphany was still unsure about what happened to her.

"Babygirl, let's not talk about it right now, I'm a take care of - " Tiara walked in giving Jay the eye.

"Yes Lord, praise God."

Jay tightened his lips and shook his head. She was taking this church thing a little too seriously. She cried as she hugged Epiphany tight and whispered a prayer of thanks. Epiphany was a bit shocked by all the praising her mother was doing.

'Damn I know I gave everybody a bit of a scare but what got into her while I was sleeping,' Epiphany thought.

Just then the doctor came in to check Epiphany's vital signs and informed her and her parents that the nurse would be in shortly to check the healing of her gun shot wound. He then asked to speak to Jay Wright and Tiara in private. They agreed and stepped outside of Epiphany's room door.

"You are aware that we ran a few test on Epiphany yesterday, right?"

"Yes we are," both parents answered.

"Good. Now for the most part, Epiphany is going to be okay. So I don't want anyone to panic, alright?" Dr. Frye said, directed his attention towards Mrs. Wright.

"Okay," she answered.

"Good! Now we did discover a bit of a problem in her right lung. It seems to be healing, just slowly. It's still very weak at this time. Therefore, she will be experiencing some difficulty with her breathing. Now I know it sounds bad, but it's not as bad as it sounds. I will be prescribing her an asthmatic pump, which will be useful to her if she should have any trouble breathing. She must carry the pump with her at all times. Now the results from the other test we took confirmed that Epiphany is suffering from partial amnesia. Meaning, she's not likely to have any recollection of any person, place or thing that has occurred in the previous hours or months leading up to the shooting."

"So Doctor does that mean that she might not ever remember who did this to her?" Tiara asked.

"Well, it's probable that she will regain her memory in spurts. It will be kind of like putting a puzzle together piece by piece. Epiphany's memory could start coming back to her tomorrow or a year from now, that part I can't say, but I will be discharging her at the end of the week. Now if you'll excuse me," said Dr. Frye as he walked off to speak to a passing nurse.

"Jay, we might not ever find out who did this to Epee," said Tiara.

"Woman, you know just as well as I do; that, that punk bastard C-god did it. I'm gonna kill him dead I swear."

"Baby, we don't know that."

"Has he been up here to see her yet, huh?"

"No but -"

"Ain't no buts about it. That's guilt right there and now the nigga's hiding out. He can't even be a man about it." Jay Wright slightly raised his voice.

"Shhhh. Okay, honey please, just let God handle it? What's important is that Epiphany is going to be fine. She's coming home with us and we can look after her. I don't need my husband going to jail because of some low-life. Are you listening to me Jay? It's not worth it."

"Not worth it to who, Tiara? Epee is our daughter and as her father it is my job to protect her by all means and that's what I'm gonna do. All that shit about God handling it, is for the birds 'cause if he was handling it, why did it happen, huh? Answer that."

"I'm sure he had his reasons, but I'm not gonna question his will," said Tiara.

"We have a lot to be thankful for. Epiphany is still here with us and we are a family and that's what you need to be focusing on."

"You and this holier than thou act is really starting to get on my nerves."

"Okay well, let me just say this Jay, we ain't getting any younger and if you want to convert back to the thug life, go right ahead, but I don't want it around me. So put that bullet in your gun and shoot it, gangsta!" Tiara might have been a changed woman but she still had a sharp tongue.

Just as Epiphany's mom headed back to the room she bumped into Keisha and Shana at the doorway.

"Hi, girls," she said.

"Hey Mrs. Wright, is Epiphany awake," asked Keisha.

"Yeah she is and I know she's gonna be happy to see you guys. But I must warn you, she has amnesia. She's not going to remember anything about the shooing or her friend's death. Please don't mention it to her because I don't want her getting upset, okay ladies?"

"Wait a minute Mrs. T, If she has amnesia how's she gonna remember us," asked Shana with a puzzled look on her face.

"She'll remember you guys because it's only part of her memory, the last couple of months that she seems to have lost."

"That's crazy. She won't remember C-God, her pregnancy or Malikai' s murder?" Keisha asked.

"Well, I hope she never remembers that no good Hinderson boy," said Mrs. Wright.

"But, what if he is the one that tried to kill her?"

"Shana, come on He did it, I know he did," Keisha had no evidence, but she felt it in her gut.

"Keisha you sound like my husband. Ya'll need to come to church with me and get some Jesus in your life. Anyway, go ahead in, I know she'll be happy to see you two. Just remember what I said."

The girls eyes widened when Mrs. Wright mention going to church and needing Jesus and they both turned to each other with the *'I don't know girl'* look on their faces. Keisha and Shana slowly pushed open Epiphany's room door not sure what to expect. They smiled when they saw her cursing out the nurses over the intercom about how cold and nasty her breakfast was.

"She's back," said Shana. Keisha ran towards Epiphany with open arms and hugged her carefully, so not to pull on her IV tubes.

"Hey ya'll what's up? Finally, my girls. Now, which one of ya'll is gonna tell me what the hell happened to me. Shana you ain't shoot me did you?" Epiphany cracked a smile.

"Oh I see you got jokes, right." Shana responded.

"Epiphany, me and Shana been coming up here to see you everyday. I'm so glad your back, you just don't know." Keisha said.

"Yes, I do. I know ya'll can't live with out me, but I gotta get the fuck up out of this hospital. Look at this cold ass oatmeal they trying to feed me and who the fuck still eats oatmeal anyway." Epiphany already back to her silly self.

"I don't know girl." Keisha agreed.

"No, but seriously; who did this to me?" Tears began to fill Epiphany's eyes and her humor turned into sadness.

"Honestly E, we don't know," answered Shana. Keisha decided it was best to keep her mouth shut because she was ready to fill in all the blanks for Epiphany.

"Keisha, where's Mali at? I know he's trying find out who did this to me, right? Does he know I'm out of a coma? Where's his ass at?" Epiphany's questions started to wear Keisha down. She burst into tears and started spilling the truth.

"Epiphany, Mali is dead. Whoever did this to you, killed him. He's gone."

"What! No, not Malikai. Why him? Why did he have to die," Epiphany cried.

"We think C-God had something to do with it." Keisha added.

"C-God?"

"Yeah Corey, Corey Hinderson. Ring any bells?" said Keisha.

"Ahhhh yeah, black Corey that use to live around our way, right?"

"Bingo!"

"But, why Keish?" Epiphany was puzzled.

"Because, you was fucking him, that's why." Shana replied.

"I was? So Mali is dead 'cause of me?" Epiphany cried.

"Epiphany, don't start blaming yourself because we don't know what Corey's reason was. He's been hating on Tucker and Mali for awhile. I honestly don't think it was you that caused of any of this." Keisha explained.

"Why can't I remember any of this?" asked Epiphany.

"Epiphany, maybe once you get better you'll remember, besides we ain't a 100% sure it was C-God. And Keisha, you make sure to tell Mrs. Wright that it was you that opened your big mouth. E, I'm glad you're okay, but just concentrate on getting better, alright."

"Keisha, I'm about to be out, I got a few things I gotta take care of, but I might be back later a'ight," said Shana.

"Okay, I'm gonna stay for the afternoon visit, since I ain't got the baby or no man to run home to." Keisha replied.

The afternoon quickly turned into evening and Keisha ended up staying until visiting hours were over. Playing catch up, she filled Epiphany in on all the drama that was going on in her life and answered whatever questions Epiphany had for her.

CHAPTER 15

Shana had a to drive out to her suppliers house in Staten Island to re-up, which was something she dreaded. She always traveled alone and made sure her transactions were quick ; she let it be known that she's always on the move so her time was limited. Once she safely made it back around the way she'd arranged to meet with Raina at various locations, so she could hit her off with work for the week. This time the meeting was at Applebee's. Shana waited in a booth, watching the entrance and her surroundings at the same time. Finally, Raina came walking in looking like Babs from "Da Band." She was wearing a Rockawear baby tee, a short jean skirt and some crispy clean tan timbs. *'Representing BK to the fullest,'* Shana thought as she watched her approach.

"What up, Cream?" Raina was the only person who still called Shana by her hustlin' name.

"Chillin'. Excuse me, waitress we ready for some drinks or something." Shana said flagging down one of the uniformed girls as she walked past.

"Okay Miss, your server will be with you in a minute," the girl replied.

"Hey, there's 500 of them things in the backpack under this table, a'ight." Shana whispered softly to Raina, getting the business part of their meeting out of the way first.

"A'ight, I'm a handle that." Raina knew the routine.

"So, what's good Raina?" Shana was ready for the gossip.

"Ain't shit, really. You know me; I'm mostly business, but some baller niggas been coming through the spot lately and they from out here in Queens. One of them niggas be acting like he checking for me too."

"Yo word, they be up in Honey's like that?" Shana asked.

"Like that kid, for the past couple of nights or so," answered Raina.

"I hear that! Get that money, just make sure it don't interfere with getting mine." Shana said flipping it back to business.

"Yo, I got you kid. I'm handling my shit."

"What's up with Silk? Where she been hiding at?"

"Man that bitch done fucked around and got her ass pregnant, again. She was still doing her thing up in Honey's until she started showing too much. But she home chilling now, out of commission for awhile," said Raina.

"So, what's up with Chasity, you seen her lately?" Shana questioned out of curiosity.

"Nah I ain't really seen her that much, but I heard she still be coming through."

"Oh that's cool." Shana said relieved.

"Excuse me, are you ladies ready to order?" asked the waiter.

Knock…Knock…Knock…

Shana woke up out of her sleep when she heard the knocking at her door. She glanced over at the clock, it read 2am.

"I hope K.C. ain't lose his damn key" she mumbled as she got out of the bed.

"Yo Sha, it's Smitty open up," he yelled.

"I'm coming. Stop knocking on my fucking door like you crazy." Shana yelled back as she cracked open the door.

"Yo what up, what up Sha?" said Smitty in a playful tone.

"K.C. ain't here Smitty." Shana snobbishly responded.

"I ain't here for him."

"Then, what do you want?"

"Yo Sha, what's up? 'cause I'm saying, you been throwing me a lot of shade lately."

"Ain't nothing up." Shana stepped back to let Smitty come inside.

"Oh, so I'm bugging out then, right?"

"Look Smitty, I don't know what you talking about."

"I'm saying Shana, every time I come through, you start rolling your eyes, huffing and puffing and shit like a nigga did something to you. All I wanna know is, what the fuck is up with all that." Smitty carried on.

"Whatever Smitty, look it's late and I'm tired, so uhh-"

"Nah, ain't no 'so ahhh!' Just let me finish."

"What do you want Smitty?" Shana rolled her eyes and let out a hard sigh making sure he knew how annoyed she was getting.

"Yo, how's what's her face doing?" Smitty said skirting around the real reason for his visit. Shana was getting defensive and stared Smitty down. She ignored his question for a few moments, assuming he was asking about Chasity to be sarcastic.

"Yo, I don't know who your talking about and honestly I don't give a fuck, so why are you wasting my time?"

"E-p-i-p-hany, that's her name," said Smitty. Shana was relieved that it wasn't Chasity he was talking about, but still decided not to give up any information.

"What is it to you?" she questioned.

"Nothing really, but since she's your friend, I just thought I'd ask. Either way that's neither here nor there 'cause that ain't why I'm here," said Smitty.

"Then what is the reason?"

"Business of course." Smitty replied.

"What business you got to discuss with me?" Shana asked with a puzzled look on her face.

"Your little business down at Honey's."

"And, what about it?" Shana snapped.

"I hear you're doing well for yourself down there."

"Oh yeah, that's what you heard?"

"Yeah that's what I'm hearing. I hear you done stepped up your game. You saw a little gold mind and handled your business, instead of lap dancing for that bullshit ass money you was making. You charging them bitches $30 dollars a pop for E, I'm really impressed."

"So what you saying, Smitty?"

"I'm *saying*, I'm trying to be on your team."

"What team? I ain't making team money." Shana argued.

"Oh really, 'caused I fucked this stripper bitch a little while ago from Honey's, who said you be making at least 10 to 15g's a week. Now, that's a nice little piece of change. So, since I know your man hates dikes and your into girls, you should be looking out for a brother. Say 40% and I'll keep your secret."

"Forty percent of what? You bugging the fuck out if you think I'm giving you my money." Shana yelled.

"A'ight then, I guess I'm a have to tell K.C. and you know how that nigga feel about that shit."

"Yo, I can't believe you Smitty. If it wasn't for me you wouldn't be making the money you making now. I helped you out and now you trying to play me. It's all good though, nigga you do dirt ,you gon' get dirt."

"Oh, I'm so scared. Just see me with that when you collect from Raina on Sunday a'ight."

"You'll get your 40%. Just go, a'ight, get out my house." Smitty slowly walked out the door past Shana, who was holding it open. She slammed it right behind him. He was kind of surprised at how easy it was to get Shana to agree to his terms.

"YOU MUTHAFUCKA." She storming into the bedroom and grabbed her cellphone. Her heart raced with anger as she dialed Raina's phone.

"What's up, Cream?" Raina answered.

"Yo, what's up with you putting my fucking business out there like that and to a nigga you don't even fucking know?"

"Yo, Cream hold up, pump your brakes for a minute. 'cause I don't know what you talking about," said Raina.

"Oh, you don't know what I'm talking about, huh?"

"Nah and you shouldn't even be coming at me like this, with bullshit?" Raina replied.

"So, you ain't fuck this kid named Smitty?" Shana asked.

"Yeah, I fucked him, but I ain't tell him shit. That's my word this what happened Check it, the nigga got a lap dance from me a couple of nights ago, right, then he starts asking me questions like, do I sell E and who I work for. So, I got a little paranoid and I backs off from the nigga. Then I start asking some of the girls some questions about him, they told me he hustled and shit was gravy with the nigga. So, I'm like cool. Now, I'm more relaxed around the nigga the next time I seen him, which was tonight. The vibe was good, so I went to the hotel with him; but I swear I ain't mention your name. That's my word on everything I love, my son all that. Did that nigga tell you some bogus shit?"

"Yep, but it's all good." Shana was pissed.

"Yo, that's my word Cream, I wouldn't do no sheisty shit like that to you and if you got that nigga's number, we can straighten this shit out now."

'*How you fuck a nigga and don't get his number,*' Shana wondered. "Nah don't even worry about it, I'll check you on Sunday."

"A'ight, see you then." Raina hung up.

Now, Shana was furious and at this point she didn't know what or who to believe. She knew somebody was ratting her out.

CHAPTER 16

Keisha spotted Tucker's BMW parked in the driveway as she pulled up to the house. She knew he was probably still pissed off at her, but just seeing his car put a smile on her face. She thought that maybe now she would have a chance to finally get some things off her chest. Keisha quickly unlocked the door, put down her keys and ran upstairs.

"Tucker," she called out, but he was nowhere in sight nor did he answer. She ran back downstairs to the living room and walked towards the kitchen, still no sign of him. Keisha heard his voice coming from the basement "Bingo." She took off towards the basement steps and quietly crept down the dimly lit stairwell. When she reached the bottom step she was greeted by the barrel of Tucker's gun. Keisha screamed and they both jumped.

"Damn Keisha, you scared the shit out of me," Tucker yelled. "You lucky I ain't one of them scared shooters, or your ass would have been a goner."

"I know, you scared me too." Keisha said catching her breath.

"What are you doing here? I thought you was suppose to be going out of town, liked I asked."

"I know, but I got classes that I'm trying to make up, Epiphany's still in the hospital, and I've been waiting to talk to you, so -"

"So, what Keisha? I told you to go for a reason. You must wanna end up in the hospital with Epiphany, or better yet like Mali. Yo, this ain't shit to be playing with and where my son at?" Tucker voice was getting louder and she could tell her was getting annoyed.

"Well ahhh, I sent him with Loretta so he could see Nana, but it's only for two weeks." Keisha answered nervously.

"Oh, so you gon' be like your mom now, huh? Shipping off your responsibilities for somebody else to take care of— is that it?"

The happiness Keisha felt when she first got home was now replaced by rage. *'How could he doubt my parenting skills? He was the one running from his family, trying to ship me off.'* His words cut her like a knife. She burst into tears.

"Tucker, how could you say that to me? I'm not like Loretta, I would never leave my son like that. I am trying my best to be a good mother, considering the kind of mother I had,. but I'm doing it. You come and go as you please, it's me that's left with all the responsibility. I have a baby to take care of and I'm trying to finish school. It's not easy."

"Keish, you right it's not easy and maybe I shouldn't of said that. Matter fact, I know I shouldn't have, but I still wish you would of went with them just to make sure my little man is good.

"I know T, but they all promised to look after him and if I had the slightest bit of doubt that Lil' T would not be properly taken care of, I would have never agreed to it. Loretta has come along way from being the mother I knew growing up. She proved it during her visit. I see the joy in her eyes when she's with our son and I honestly believe that she won't disappoint me this time.

"A'ight Keish, I hope your right." At this point, Keisha no longer wanted to discuss him and her. It didn't seem like she matter to Tucker anymore. He made it very clear to her every time they talked that his only concern was their son. She stared at Tucker. His clear caramel skin was so beautiful, and his silky black hair waves looked like the ocean. She thought back to how fine he was when they first met and as the years passed he only got finer. She loved him deeply, with all her heart and would do anything for a second chance. Unfortunately, the ball was in Tucker's court. Keisha headed back up stairs to the kitchen, loaded the dishwasher and decided to get dinner started. She figured that maybe a home cooked meal might soften Tucker's mood, assuming it might of been awhile since he had one. Usually, if it wasn't Keisha or Mom Dukes cooking, he wouldn't fuck with it. Keisha made fried chicken, rice and steamed broccoli. As soon as the aroma filled the air, Tucker came running.

"Damn Keish, what's that you cooking?" He said as he rummaged through the pots.

"Help yourself, T. I'm gonna go take a shower and lay down."

"What, you not gon' eat?"

"Nah, I made that for you."

"Thanks, good looking out." Tucker piled his plate with everything and went back to the basement.

After Keisha showered she threw on a large t-shirt and hopped into bed. All type of thoughts ran through her mind. Mainly the sex tape and how foolish it was for her to do what she did, not to mention doing it a second time. After beating herself up over and over again, she thought about how ironic it was that outside of Epiphany, Shana, and her classmate, Simone, none of the girls at the party had contacted her to see how she was doing. What was even stranger was how Simone called her several times but her other classmate, Lea, didn't. Especially since she felt much closer to Lea. They had three classes together and Lea hadn't even bothered to see why Keisha hadn't been to school in weeks. It all just seemed a bit suspect to Keisha and the more she thought about it, the more her fingers starting to point at Lea, who put the whole shin-dig together. Still, how would she get to the bottom of it all. That question boggled her mind until finally, she fell asleep.

About an hour into Keisha's sleep, Tucker came into the bedroom. He turned on the night light and watched her. *'Damn Keish why you had to do me like this. I love you so much, you just don't know how bad you hurt me girl,'* he thought. Keisha was looking real good to him as she laid on her stomach. The covers were down by her feet, where she had kicked them, and from the way her t-shirt rested on her ass, Tucker could tell she wasn't wearing any panties. His dick started to get hard—real hard. He didn't know if he wanted to get back with her, but he knew he wanted her now. He took off his jeans and slowly crawled into bed behind her. Placing his fingers between her legs he began to finger fuck her slowly, just the way she liked it. Keisha started to moan and move to the rhythm of Tucker's fingers as her juices flowed heavily. She was so horny, it felt like she was going to explode. Turning over she whispered, "Please fuck me T, I want you so bad." Tucker wanted to fuck her just as bad, but first he leaned over and grabbed a condom from the pocket of his jeans. When Keisha realized that he was putting on a condom she got offended, because for one; she was on birth control and two; in the seven years they were together, he never wore one before. So, the fact that he felt the need to wear one now made her wonder, which one of them he felt the need to protect. Her mind started telling her 'no', but her body was still screaming a strong 'yes', that she couldn't ignore. Tucker started out with slow deep strokes as he kissed her neck and breasts. It had been awhile since the two made love to each other that they both forgot how good they felt to one another. Tucker then started to pound her pussy once he located Keisha's spot. He always could tell when he was hitting it by the way her pussy would start to pulsate on the tip of his dick. Keisha knew that once she threw it back and tightened her vagina muscles it would be a wrap for Tucker. As they both began to cum, Keisha felt like she had died and gone to paradise. She saw the sun, the moon, the mountains and the rivers, it was heaven just like the Az Yet once sang. But, before she knew it the lovemaking was over and Tucker had rolled over, turning his back towards her and drifted off to sleep. Keisha smiled as she snuggled up close, burying her head into his back. She was happy just to have him next to her again and hoped that maybe, just maybe, tonight was the start of a clean slate and he was ready to forgive her, come home and put all this mess behind them. She closed her eyes and doze back off to sleep with high hopes.

CHAPTER 17

C-God was in Virginia staying with his Puerto Rican Mami, Marisa. He met her about four years ago, she was one of his out-of-town pieces. Marisa was a bit of a big girl, but had a real pretty face and had three bad ass kids. She also had a large appetite for the nose candy (cocaine) and was a real freak-a-leak (as Petey Pueblo would say) once she got her hands on some. Crazy niggas ran up in her but couldn't front on her 'cause she had some good ass pussy, sucked a mean dick, took it in the ass and made the hell out of some Arroz con Pollo (chicken and rice). Shit, what more could a nigga ask for. C-god always did like Spanish chicks. He felt they were pleasers and knew how to take care of a man. It didn't matter whether you was rich or poor, if they loved you, they were loyal and he admired that.

C-god didn't quite hit rock bottom until he found out about his parents. That was the shit that took him over the edge. At this point the large amounts of cocaine he was sniffing no longer numbed him so he started free-basing it. He went from pulling in 50g's a week to losing his right-hand man, having the Feds on his ass, and now his parents were dead. All that sent him into a rage of fury. He couldn't even pay his last respects at their funeral because the undercovers had it surrounded in hopes of his arrival. That hurt the most. C-God broke down and cried like a bitch because he could no longer endure the pain he was feeling. He called Tanya, his newest baby momma, and asked her if she would pay her respects for him. Tanya agreed, even though she had never met his parents. She figured that with C-God being the youngest of four, he had to have shared a close relationship with his parents. She sympathized with him deeply. Tanya knew that some shit went down, but she didn't know any details and she also knew not pry. Before saying goodbye, C-god promised to try and meet up with her soon to explain everything, but not once did he mention their son.

CHAPTER 18

The news about Malikai really devastated Epiphany. As far as her memory was concern, she thought they had never stopped seeing each other. She recalled the weird dream she had when she was in the hospital. Over and over, she questioned it's meaning. *'Was Mali saying goodbye.'*

On top of that, Epiphany had to get use to living with her parents again—something she hadn't done since she was 18, which was almost five years ago. It hadn't even been a full week yet and already they were driving her up the walls with the questions: *"Epee are you okay?", "Do you have your pump?", "Where are you going?"*

"If you guys would have paid this much attention to me growing up I could've avoided a lot of trouble." She'd constantly say. Her dad wasn't that bad, but Epiphany could barely pee in peace without her mom breathing down her back. The only time she did manage to get some peace was when Tiara left for church, that is, after she failed to convince Epiphany to tag along. Epiphany could not believe how involved her mom really was with the church thing. She was still giving Jay the cold shoulder for his determination to find C-God Jay was beginning to think she had another man because he always thought church was only on Sundays, whereas his wife was faithfully attending every Sunday, Wednesdays and Friday evening service. It got to the point where he would smell her panties once she took them off, just to make sure they didn't have a sex or latex scent.

"Alone at last," Epiphany sighed relief. It was one of those evenings when Tiara had church and Jay happened to be out in the streets. Epiphany hadn't fully recovered yet, but she needed to go back to her place, she had to, in search of some answers. She grabbed her cellphone and car keys and out the door she went. Once she reached her apartment, she instantly spotted a 'for rent' sign in the window. She got out the car and attempted to use her key, but the didn't work. She walked around to the side of the two family house and peaked through the her bedroom window, it was empty from what she could see. "Where the fuck is my shit." She screamed as she walked back to her car. Epiphany grabbed her cellphone and dial the number on the 'for rent' sign.

"Hello?" a man's voice answered.

"Yes, is this Mr. Raymond?" She was obviously aggravated.

"Ahhh, yeah. Who am I speaking with?" Mr. Raymond responded back.

"This is Epiphany Wright, I was renting your 1st floor apartment over here off of Guy R Brewer Ave. and I need to know where my stuff is."

"Well young lady, I don't know where your stuff is, but I do know that a gentleman claiming to be your father paid me the remaining balance of your lease and took your belongings with him."

"Oh, okay then, thanks." Epiphany hit the end call button on her phone. She sat parked in front of the house staring off into space when suddenly a quick glimpse came to her. She saw Malikai's truck pull up in front of her apartment, then he was sitting on her couch. What Epiphany saw next caused her to have an asthma attack. She saw herself standing in front of Mali, pointing her gun at him and in one last flash the gun went off. Wheezing and gasping for air, she searched the car for her asthma pump, but only found a brown paper bag instead. With tears pouring down her face she quickly placed the bag over her mouth, then inhaled and exhaled until she gained control of her breathing. "Oh my god, I killed him" she whispered.

Epiphany replayed Mali's murder in her mind for days, but it just didn't make sense to her. *"If I killed Malikai then who shot me? Was it in self -defense?"* The same two questions kept popping up in her head. She couldn't eat or sleep since her revelation, she needed answers. If her father was the last one in her apartment she felt it was time to ask him some questions.

"Daddy, listen. I really need to talk to you."

"What's up Epee?" Jay Wright responded.

"Are the police trying to find out what really happened?"

"I doubt it, as far as they're concerned your friend is just one less nigga they got to worry about. The truth will surface sooner or later and when it does I'll take care of it, meanwhile don't stress yourself out Epee."

"But Daddy, you don't understand, I need to know what happened." Epiphany said slightly raising her voice.

"Epee, look I don't know what to tell you. I tried to warn you about the company you was keeping, but you didn't want to hear it."

"Daddy did anything look suspicious in my apartment, like my locks? Were they broken or anything?"

"No, besides the blood stained couch and a busted up stereo nothing was out of place."

"My gun Daddy, the nine you gave me, was it still in my closet? Epiphany continued to question.

"Nah, I ain't see no gun."

"Do you think the police found it?" Epiphany asked.

"Hell no, you kidding me. If so, they would've had a field

day prosecuting you, especially since you're my daughter." Jay Wright said, checking his Rolex for the time.

"Epee look, I have to go and take care of something, you gon be a'ight?"

"Yeah, I'm cool." Epiphany answered disappointedly. Her father's answers weren't much help.

CHAPTER 19

"I feel so stupid. I can't believe Tucker just fucked me and left without saying a word, like I'm some whore off the street or something." It was day two since they hit skins and still no Tucker insight, not even a courtesy call. Keisha tried reaching him on his cell, but after leaving several messages, she gave up. At that moment, there was only one word to describe how Keisha was feeling—*played. 'If this is Tucker's way of making me feel like shit on the bottom of his shoe, well damn it, he's done it.'* Tears began to run down her face and the feeling of loneliness came over her. *'Maybe he's seeing someone else,'* she thought. *'All the signs are right in my face; he won't answer my calls, he can't be living out of a hotel all this time and he fucked me with a condom. I guess to keep from bringing my scent home to his new girl. That has to be it."* Keisha cried out, her assumptions made everything seem all too clear. She got out of bed and started packing all of Tucker's belongings. "If you want to be with somebody else that's fine, but you won't do it here," she screamed out, while throwing all his things into garbage bags. "I'm done with the apologies and making an ass out of myself over and over again." Keisha struggled as she dragged the bags down the steps and left them by the front door. Then, she dialed Tucker, who of course didn't answer. "Tucker this is Keisha and since you haven't bothered to return any of my calls, don't. Just come and get your stuff, it's already packed and waiting by the door. So the hard part is over. Goodbye." Keisha exhaled as she plopped down to the floor and new tears began to fall replacing the dry ones. She took a moment to collect her thoughts, but all she kept asking herself was, *"Damn, how could I be so stupid? Why did I do it? I know he's not coming back."* Still holding the phone in her hand she decide to call and check on her son.

"Hello?" answered her grandmother.

"Hi Nana, it's me Keisha."

"Hi Keisha, baby, how's things up that way?"

"Fine, is my mother around?"

"No honey, she took the baby to the park. Keisha he is so precious."

"Thank you, I miss him so much, but I'm gonna a need a little more time to myself, so can you please tell her to call me when she gets back?"

"I sure will and listen honey I heard about them problems you having up there with that man of yours. Don't let him get you down -you hear? I'm praying for you. And don't be no fool, you make sure you putting away some of that money he got - you hear me? Take as much time as you need, don't worry about this beautiful little boy of yours, he's being well taking care of-you hear?"

"Thanks Nana."

"Alright now baby," said Nana, before hanging up the phone.

CHAPTER 20

Shana was tight about having to pay Smitty that kind of hush money. Besides, she was starting to wonder if it was even worth it. K.C. didn't even bring his black ass home last night and yet she was paying his right-hand man a cut of the money she made. Shana wanted to get her mind off the stress in her life, she needed to throw on her *'fuck him dress'*, head to the club, get her drink on, dance and just have some fun for a change. She called Keisha to see if she was down. Clubbing was something Keisha hadn't done in years, so it might help her get her mind off Tucker.

"Hello?" Keisha picked up after the fifth ring.

"Damn Keish, I was about to hang the fuck up, what you doing?"

"Nothing girl, just finished surfing the net for a job and waiting for Tucker to come and get his things?"

"Job, what you talking about? Tucker's moving out?"

"He needs to, I packed all his stuff and told him to come get it, so that means I'm going to need a job, so I won't go through the money I've been saving."

"Shit is that bad, huh?"

"Yep, I'm only fooling myself thinking he'll take me back. It's obvious he don't want to be with me anymore, so I might as well face it."

"Did he say that?"

"No, but his action say it. I can't even be mad at him because if he did what I did, I probably wouldn't want him neither."

"Keish, you know what your problem is, you need to stop feeling sorry for yourself and get out the house and have some fun. Fuck that nigga, let's go out and get our club on or something girl, do you for a change."

" I don't know," she said hesitantly.

"Keisha, what you mean you don't know? The baby ain't there and neither is Tucker. So come on, let's have some fun, PLEASE," Shana said putting the beg on. Keisha sat on that thought a few moments longer, it *was* time to get out, have a little fun and focus on doing her.

"Alright I'm down, let me see if Epiphany wants to come too."

"Epiphany! Do you think she's well enough to go to a club?" Shana asked.

"Yeah she's good, it'll be like old times, just the three of us."

"Cool, I'll check back with you around ten o'clock."

"Just come over." Keisha hung up with Shana and dialed Epiphany.

"Praise the lord," answered Mrs. Wright.

"Ahhhh, h-e-l-l-o?" said Keisha.

"Yes, who would you like to speak to?"

"Mrs. Wright."

"Yes."

"Oh hi, is Epiphany there? It's Keisha."

"Hi sweetie, hold for a moment okay? Epiphany, Keisha's on the phone," she yelled.

"Hello?" said Epiphany, picking up the phone.

"Hey girl, what's up?" Keisha asked.

"Girl, my moms is driving me nuts."

"Why, what's wrong?"

"She done went Christian crazy. Every five minutes she's talking about God or trying to get me to go to church with her. She even bought me a bible and get this, she plays church music all fucking day now."

"Well, what does your father say?" Keisha asked.

"What can he say, she ain't even speaking to him, for whatever reason. But, I'm guessing it has something to do with her new found religion. And that's not even the half of it, she told me that the name Epiphany meant some type of celebration for Christ."

"What?" Keisha questioned in disbelief.

"Yes girl, that's it for me. I have to get the hell out of here, she's too much for me. I'll never get my memory back living here." Epiphany laughed.

"I got an idea, why don't you come stay with me?" Keisha suggested.

"Are you serious? What about Tucker?"

"I packed his stuff, girl." Keisha said in a disappointed tone and sucked her teeth before continuing. "Besides it ain't like he's ever here anyway, so he might as well take his belongings with him, right? Anyway don't worry about him, just come on, okay?"

"Check you out, finally putting your foot down. Even thought you did wait until you fucked up to do it, but at least you doing it. Anyway we'll talk about it when I get there."

"No, we'll talk about it tomorrow 'cause me, you, and Shana hanging out tonight."

"Oh, for real. I'm with that, I'll see you in a minute then."

CHAPTER 21

Epiphany was so anxious to move out of her parents' house, that she didn't put much thought into her decision to move with Keisha. All she knew was she wanted out and wasn't quite ready to get a place of her own just yet. Epiphany also knew that even though she was grown, her Mom would make a big deal about her leaving, so she decided that easing her way out would be her best move. *'I'll just pack enough for a few nights, tell them I'm chilling with Keisha for a few days and then gradually get the rest of my things,'* Epiphany thought as she plotted out her plan. She packed fast and did just that, she told her parents it was only for a few nights. Tiara was uneasy about her spending the night out so soon after what had happened and bearing in mind her condition, just as Epiphany expected her to her to be. She already had her, *"I'm 22 soon to be 23, which means I'm not asking permission, I'm just letting you guys know where I'll be"* speech prepared.

"Baby she is grown, besides it's only for a couple of nights." Jay Wright assuring Tiara that Epiphany would be fine. It was a done deal, Epiphany was out the door and in her car as soon as she said her rushed goodbyes. She turned on the radio and blasted Hot 97 all the way to Keisha's house. Keisha rushed to the door, kicking Tucker's bags further to the side to make room for Epiphany to enter.

"Hey girl!" she screamed full of excitement as they rocked side to side hugging each other tightly.

"Thanks, Keish, for letting me chill here."

"Girl please! Don't even mention it, you know your like a sister to me, so cut it out and get in here. Shana should be here around ten."

"Damn, what's all this?" Epiphany asked referring to the bags by the door.

"Tucker's stuff. What you thought I was playing? I think it's really over between us 'cause he don't act like he feeling me at all."

"Keish, he's probably just wants to make you suffer for a little while, that's all."

"Oh, so I guess that's why he fucked me the other night, fell asleep with his back turned and then got up and left and hasn't spoke to me since."

"Shit at least you got some, I can't even remember the last time I had some dick. I just hope for your sake you put it on his ass and fucked him good, 'cause if you did, he ain't going nowhere," laughed Epiphany.

"You know I did girl!" Keisha said wondering if her sex was as good to him as his was to her. "Come on let me take you to your room 'cause we need to be getting ready."

CHAPTER 22

The trio was back together again. It had been a while since all three of the girls hit the club together, so of course they had to represent. Epiphany was dressed in an all black halter top cat suit by Sean John (Not the Sean John hood shit you find in Monies or Macy's, this was P.Diddy's exclusive runway shit-ONLY for the grown and sexy). She wore her hair straight back and it flowed nicely down her back. She applied a glitter gloss to her lips along with an earth tone eye shadow that complimented her slanted eyes. After all her last minute primping, she slid her freshly French pedicured feet into her Gucci sandals and was ready for whatever. Keisha was dressed a little too conservative for Epiphany's taste— a knee-length Chanel skirt with a buttoned up blouse by Donna Karen. Sister needed some serious help.

"Oh hell no, you ain't going with me looking like that. We're going to a club not a fucking job interview." Epiphany snapped.

"I know, but I don't have nothing else to wear." Keisha whined. Epiphany dug down in her bag and pulled out a fitted little dress by BCBG.

"Here put this on," she said throwing it at Keisha. The dress was a little too short and sexy for Keisha ,but she didn't want to hear Epiphany's plain Jane jokes, so she decided to just rolled with it. Epiphany took care of her hair and make-up and Keisha threw on some Stiletto mid- way calf boot from Aldo to at least hide some of her legs. Shana arrived at a quarter past ten. She was looking cute as well, wearing a black and white sheer shirt that hung off her right shoulder, black stretch boot-cut pants and a pair of heels. She wasn't really into all that name brand shit, to her it was the person that made the clothes not the other way around. So while chicks were out there trying to keep up with the Jones' (like her mother, Ms. Pat, would say)—spending three or four hundred for an outfit—Shana's cost about eighty bucks and she still looked good. Epiphany was glad that both of her girls finally had their own rides now, but she got a little jealous when Keisha volunteered to be the designated driver with her brand new, fully loaded X5 with spinners.

"Keisha, when did you get this." she asked.

"Oh Tucker bought it, but he gave it to me right before all the drama started, why you like it?"

"Yeah it's a'ight, but he should of got you the silver one though." Shana rolled her eyes noticing Epiphany's hateration, but kept quite about it because she was determined to have a good time tonight. The girls made it to Club Suede around midnight. They headed straight for the bar. The club was kind of empty at first, but didn't take long to fill up with all kinds of people; black, white, Asian, you name it and they were up in there partying it up. Suede was also a well-known hang out spot for the baller/celebrities. That particular night, P. Diddy and his entourage was up in there along with Cameron Diaz and Justin Timberlake, who danced the night away in the VIP section. Epiphany, of course being the diva she only knew how to be, wanted nothing less then VIP status, plus she wanted Puffy to noticed her and how good she looked in his Sean John design. She started by making eye contact with one of the big body bouncers in front the velvet ropes. His arms were folded and he didn't seem to pay her much attention. She walked over to him and bluntly asked, "Ahhh, can you let me and my girls through please?"

Without even looking down at her he replied, "Nah shorty I can't."

"Come on, I said please. I'll give you my number." Epiphany said with a flirtatious smile. He gave her a dirty look. Disappointed and bothered by the bouncer's rejection, Epiphany stormed off and head back over to Shana and Keisha, who stood holding their drinks, waiting patiently for her to signal them over to VIP.

"That muthafucka got to be gay," she yell out to them over the loud music.

"Or maybe you lost your touch." Shana laughed at her snide remark.

"Never that." Epiphany didn't find the humor at all.

"Oh come you guys, let's just have some fun." Keisha was the mediator as always.

"Yeah, lets." Shana rolled her eyes.

"Keisha just give me my drink. You and her go have fun, I'ma go stand over there" Epiphany said pointing towards the VIP section.

"You sure?" asked Keisha.

"Yessss, go," Epiphany yelled as she headed back over to the ropes. She was certain she'd get up in VIP. The DJ was putting it down with the music. The fellas were hawking the females like vultures, it didn't take long for Keisha and Shana to find dance partners. Epiphany sipped on her drink and checked out the scene carefully. Suddenly, she felt a tap on her shoulder. Slowly, she turned to her left and there stood a six-foot-four, nicely built, caramel brown complexion brother with light eyes.

"What's your name, shorty?" he asked with a killer smile. Jackpot bells went off in Epiphany's heads when she looked down and saw he was standing on the other side of the ropes in VIP, where she needed to be. She smiled at him, damn near showing all her pearly whites.

"Epiphany."

"Epiphany?" he repeated.

"Ugh huh."

"That's nice, it's different." Epiphany smiled again, moving seductively to the music and taking a sip from her glass.

"What you drinking."

"A mimosa," she replied in a sexy, but girlish kind of tone.

"Oh word, so why don't you come chill with me and have another one?"

She smiled some more, "Okay."

"Yo, Dude let shorty through." he said to the bouncer. Epiphany gave the bouncer a mean *'you should of let me through the first time'* look as he shook his head and reluctantly unhooked the rope to let her through. She walked over to her new friend's table and he introduced her to four of his boys and two girls that looked like video hoes with all their assets hanging out.

"Okay, I know their names, but I don't know yours," she said. He gave her a dumbfounded look like she was suppose to know who he was.

"That's 'cause you ain't ask."

"I'm asking you now," Epiphany replied.

"Wild."

"Wild what?"

"No, that's my name," he said.

"Oh, okay!"

The two hit it off so well, she forgot all about the celebs in

VIP and her girls. Wild entertained her with his conversation, jokes and plenty of Veuve Clicquot mimosas refills. Epiphany didn't find him all that attractive, as a matter of fact on a scale of one to ten she'd rate him a flat five, but deep pockets and a free-hearted spirit could easily put him in the eight spot, especially if the dick was good. A big nigga like him had to be equipped with a 'get-up-in-ya-guts' size dick, meaning 12 inches or more. She learned that he was a music producer and owned his own company called Wild One Productions, with quite a few hits under his belt. Epiphany felt kind of bad for not knowing who he was from the jump. She loved the limelight niggas; Jay Z, 50 Cent and P. Diddy, but she could've give a fuck about the behind the scenes nigga laying the tracks, *until now*.

"Epiphany!" Keisha was standing next to the security guard.

"Yo, is that your friend calling you?" Wild asked. Epiphany turned around and noticed Keisha signaling her to come over.

"Yeah that's one of them," she said getting up to see what Keisha wanted.

"Nah, hold up a minute." Wild pulled Epiphany back down in the seat. "Yo, Homes," he called out to the bouncer "Let her through."

"Sorry Man, I can't let no more through right now," the bouncer replied.

"That's alright, let me just go see what she wants, okay?" Epiphany said to Wild as she got up and walk over to Keisha.

"What's up girl?"

"Nothing, but we're ready to go."

"Already?" Epiphany said looking down at her diamond face Rolie, which only read three am.

"Yeah, I'm tired and I think Shana had too much to drink." Epiphany sucked her teeth and let out a hard sigh.

"Okay, just give me five minutes."

"Alright, we'll be waiting by the exit." Epiphany walked back over to Wild with an agitated look on her face.

"What's up?" he asked.

"Nothing, I should of drove my own car that's all, but since I didn't, I have to go."

"Ahhh come on, you can't be serious. Our vibe is too good for you go now."

"Yeah, but my girls are ready now."

"So then let them go and I'll take you home."

The offer sounded good, but Epiphany didn't want to seem too thirsty, besides the last time she was with a guy she ended up with a bullet in her chest, so it was best that she played it safe.

"Nah I'm gonna go, but why don't you take my number."

"Oh no doubt, hold up let me put it in my phone." Wild said pulling out his phone. "Okay now what is it?" Epiphany recited her number while he punched the number keys on his phone and repeated them back to her. "A'ight sexy I'ma holla at you." Epiphany blushed as she said goodnight.

"Damn these bitches get on my nerves," she mumbled under her breath, making her way to the exit.

CHAPTER 23

It was six in the morning when the all the yelling and screaming woke Epiphany up out of barely two hours of sleep. She hopped up out of bed, cracked the bedroom door and stuck her head out to hear what the fuss was about. Being miss nosey, she wasn't satisfied with just the earshot she had on Keisha and Tucker's argument, she wanted to see what was going on as well. Epiphany tippy-toed over to the stairs and peeked down into the living room. She still wasn't able to get a clear view, but she could hear the them better.

"Who told you to pack my stuff up, Keish?" Not giving her a chance to answer his question he continued, "Look just unpack my things and put everything back where it belongs." Tucker tried to rationalize without getting loud.

"I ain't unpacking nothing." Keisha said shrugging her shoulders. "I want you to take it and go, since you don't want to be with me anymore—leave."

"You got some fucking nerve," laughed Tucker, pausing in disbelief. "I don't believe you. You walk around here acting like I'm the bad guy, Keisha, but if I'm not mistaken you're the one that went out and fucked some gay-ass stripper nigga. You're crazy if you think I'm leaving *my* house. You better be lucky I let you stay here."

"What! You can't make me leave, my name is on the deed too." Keisha said.

95

"I don't give a shit, my money paid for this right here, so act up if you want to and word to my son, I'll burn this bitch down and neither one of us'll live in it. I ain't trying to hear all that shit about your name. The only reason why you still here is because of my little man. You played me and ain't no way in hell I could forgive some shit like that."

This was the first time Tucker had ever spoke about how he felt about what she did. He had finally confirmed it—it was over.

"The only reason he lets me stay is because of the baby huh," Keisha said to herself.

Tucker still loved her, but there was no way he could get past what she did, not now anyway. It might have been different if he heard that she fucked around, but seeing her get fucked by another dude, especially a stripper left tainted thoughts of her in his mind. Watching her cry, made him feel bad, but in all reality she did it to herself.

"Tucker, I'm sorry, baby. Please tell me you still want me, please say we can work this out." Keisha sobbed. "I'll do anything. I love you so much. You're the only man I ever loved and will ever love. I can't live without you" Keisha poured her heart out to Tucker as he sat on the couch with his head down trying to take everything she was saying into consideration. There was a moment of silence between the two. While Keisha waited for Tucker to say something, he was at a loss for words. Part of him wanted to push his pride to the side and wrap his arms around her waist, hold her tight, tell her how much he loved her and tell her 'Yes, I forgive you.' The other part of him wanted to wrap his hands around her neck, squeeze the dear life out of her and express the hate he felt towards her for playing him like she did.

Meanwhile while Epiphany continued to get her ear hustle on at the head of the steps she too waited impatiently for one of the two to respond. Her heart went out to Tucker as she watched him closely and imagined what her life might have been like if she would of gotten with him instead of Mali. Tucker was fine and she envied the kind of relationship Keisha had with him.

They were exclusive and he adored her. So she couldn't understand why she or anyone else for that matter would jeopardize perfection to get dicked down by some cornball with muscles. Even though she couldn't remember exactly what happened, she knew without a doubt that her strong influence on Keisha could have prevented her from making such a big mistake. Still looking down at the hardwood floor, Tucker shook his head and finally broke his silence.

"Keish, I can't...I can't fuck with you like that. You can stay here if you want, as long as you want, just be a good mother to my son that's all I ask. I'll still pay the bills, take care of my son and do what I gotta do. But, this is my house and I'll come and go as I please, so don't be bringing no niggas up in here. You got that?"

Keisha didn't answer, she just stood in front of him with her arms folded, tapping her feet while the tears continuously roll down her face.

"Go, get you some rest, you can put my stuff back when you wake up." Tucker got up and walked out the front door.

"Keisha?" Epiphany called out as she stepped down to the middle of the stairs, where she saw Keisha balled up on the couch crying. Keisha didn't answer.

CHAPTER 24

When Shana got home K.C. was in the bed knocked out sleeping. The eight apple martini's she had at the club had her stumbling all over bedroom, while trying to undress. Easing herself into bed, she stared at K.C. with disgust while he slept. Considering he chose not to come home the night before she was furious. She wanted to wake him up and lash out at his ass the best way she knew how. But, it was six in the morning and him being the nigga he was would only flip it, wanting to know why she was just getting in and where she had been. She contemplated whether or not she should take it there. Hopping up out of bed Shana was looking for a fight. Creeping over to K.C.'s side of the bed, where his pants rested on the floor, she kneeled down and checked his pockets in search of condoms or anything that might indicate that he was fucking around. Deep down inside she didn't want to believe that he was, but she wasn't about to sleep on him neither. Shana then took his cell phone from it's charger and headed to the bathroom with it. She closed the door and turned on the faucet to drown out the sound of the keys on the phone as she pushed them to check the call history of all his incoming and out going calls. *'No incoming or out going calls all day, bullshit.'* She found it ironic that no data appeared on the screen. From that she assumed he was guilty of foul play. Shana stormed back to the bedroom and threw K.C.'s phone at him, scaring him up out of his sleep.

"Bitch what the fuck is wrong with you?" He yelled.

"You muthafucka, that's what. Where the fuck did you stay at last night?"

"Man, come on with all that bullshit. I tell you one thing, you throw something else at me like that again and watch me beat the shit out of you." K.C. threatened.

"Fuck you nigga, you better go beat on the ho you was with last night. And why the fuck you erase all the calls off your phone, you sneaky bastard?" K.C. jumped up and grabbed Shana by her throat pulling her down to the bed.

"You noisy drunk-ass bitch, keep your hands off my shit! The only reason I did that, was to see if your sneaky ass be snooping through my shit." Shana struggled on the bed as she pulled at his hands hoping to get him to unloosen the tight grip he had around her neck.

"Get the fuck off of me," she cried.

"You gon' shut the fuck up, right?" K.C. asked before he let her go noticing how red her face had turned along with the tears that were streaming down the sides of her face. He released her and started to laugh. "I bet you'll stay out my shit now, won't you?" K.C. said.

"K.C., just leave me alone." Shana whispered. massage her neck.

"Ahhh, come here," he said pulling her towards him, "I'm sorry, but you did hit me first" K.C. pleaded his case as he began to fondle Shana's breast.

"K.C., stop it."

"What the fuck you mean stop it, this is mine right here." He grabbed in between her legs. "Right?" Looking dead in her face, he waited for the correct answer to come out her mouth.

"Yeah, but-"

"A'ight then. Ain't no buts."

"K.C. for real, all jokes aside, are you fucking around on me?"

"Yo, why you bugging the fuck out with all this bullshit." K.C. said shaking his head, still avoiding her question.

"I knew you was. You can't even answer the fucking question." Shana said pushing his arms off of her so she could pull herself up.

"Sha, where you think you going? I ain't fucking no other bitch. Stop tripping and chillout, a'ight?"

"Yeah a'ight," Shana agreed, still not convinced, but she knew it was a no win situation.

"Good, now here, taste daddy. Make a nigga feel good since you woke me up," he said wiggling his hardness from side to side.

Later that afternoon, Shana was still sleeping when K.C. came in the bedroom already dressed and smelling like weed. He tugged roughly on her shoulder.

"Yo Sha, wake up. Come on, get up and fix me and the fellas something to eat."

"Stop. Come on, no. I'm tired." Shana barked, pulling the covers up over her head.

"Yo, get up and feed a nigga. That's my word yo, you slipping on your wifely duties. You don't do shit around this muthafucka, GET UP!" he yelled snatching the covers off of her.

"You get on my fucking nerves." Shana sucked her teeth, put on her sweats and headed for the kitchen.

"I don't give a fuck, after you feed me you can leave. And yo, I don't eat no pork." Shana didn't bother to respond, he knew damn well that she didn't fuck with swine no more. K.C. was nc

doubt an asshole but part of his performance was for the bene-
fit of his boys Smitty, and some new jack nigga named Ness,
who were sitting in her living room. They seemed to find his dis-
respect towards her entertaining.

Shana was still paying Smitty and still trying to figure out
how to get out of that situation. She couldn't stand him and K.C.
was on her shit list too. She didn't know shit about this new cat
Ness, except he was paid, and rumor had it he's the one that ran
C-God out of town. But one thing was for certain her vibes never
lie and if he hung with those two he was up to no good as well.

CHAPTER 25

"Keisha, I know you ain't gon' keep moping around here like it's the end of the fucking world. You got to get it together girl. Come on, get up. Your hanging out with me tonight." Epiphany said.

"No, I'm really not up for it."

"Keisha, how long are you gonna sit here feeling so damn sorry for yourself, that you can't even get up and go wash your ass? You need to get up, take a nice hot bath and come on out and have some fun. You don't even have to worry about finding anything to wear 'cause I already took care of that at the mall earlier. So come on."

"Epiphany, where are we suppose to be going?"

"Out!"

"Out, where?"

"To Lotus." Epiphany started pulling the covers off of Keisha.

"On a Monday night?"

"Yeah girl, that's the night it be jumping. And damn, do it matter? You act like you got a job to be at in the morning or something. What's with all the questions, anyway? You ain't got shit to do, but sit up in here and be crazy depressed. You might as well get use to going out and meeting people, I'm pretty sure Tucker's doing it.

"I guess your right. Shoot, let me see that outfit." Keisha said absorbing all of Epiphany's advice.

"That's my girl. Now go wash your stinking ass *'cause we gon' party like it's your birthday,'* tonight" Epiphany started singing a verse from 'In the Club' by 50 Cent.

That night was just the beginning. Epiphany and Keisha were doing the club thing hard. Every night of the week there was something popping off in the "City that Never Sleeps", and those two where there. Mondays was Lotus or Suite 16, Missions on Tuesday, Wednesdays, Club Show, the Cherry Lounge on Thursdays and on Friday and Saturday it's whatever, 'cause just about every club had it going on. Shana kicked it with them a few times, but like always she was off doing her own thing. For Keisha, getting her party on was just what the doctor ordered. She couldn't remember the last time she had so much fun. She even arranged for her son to stay in Atlanta for at least two more weeks, and the more she got her club on the less she thought about Tucker.

One night they were out at this spot named Cream. Epiphany noticed these three guys at the bar buying Hennessy Privilege by the bottle *'Yeah, this is Privilege too,'* she thought since they all seemed to be checking her out so hard. It got to a point were their stares started making her feel uncomfortable, like maybe they knew her or something. Then she saw Keisha walk over and talk to one of the guys. *'Okay', now's the perfect time to go over and find out what's really good.'* Epiphany pranced over to the bar where they all were standing.

"Girl, I was looking all over for you," said Epiphany, putting her arm around Keisha.

"You was? Oh, I was in that damn bathroom on that long ass line waiting to pee. Anyway you remember K.C. right?" asked Keisha.

04

"His face looks familiar, but I can't really recall where I know him from."

"Girl this is Shana's man, you don't remember him." Keisha questioned. Epiphany rolled her eyes and gave Keisha the '*Hello stupid, that's what amnesia means*' look.

"Oh damn, sorry girl. I forgot all about that." Keisha realizing what that look meant.

"Hi K.C., I'm sure Shana told you about my little accident right?"

"Yeah, she ran that by me. How you making out though?" K.C. questioned.

"I'm okay, thanks for asking." Epiphany answered.

Meanwhile, Smitty and Ness kept their backs turned to avoid any chances of her remembering them. Although they had already been aware of Epiphany's memory loss, they didn't want to take any chances.

"Yo B, that bitch really don't remember us," Ness whispered with a boyish giggle.

"Man, you believe that shit?" said Smitty, not easily buying into that amnesia act.

"Nah, that bitch don't remember! She got more then a good look at me, to recognize who the fuck I am, plus that weak ass nigga C said my name. She badder than a muthafucka though."

"Yeah, I use to fuck with her, the pussy good too. Word up, I can definitely vouch for that shit," laughed Smitty. "Shit, matter fact nigga I can drink to that," he added.

"Yo, you a funny muthafucka," laughed Ness.

"Where's Shana?" Keisha asked K.C.

"I don't know. She was home when I left. I'm surprised she ain't with ya'll."

"So, K.C. whose your friends, 'cause they were staring me down when I was standing over there by myself. Now I'm over here and they act like they're to scared to turn around and say hello." Epiphany said, being as blunt and bold as always.

"Oh, those my niggas—they ain't never scared. Right fellas tell this pretty lady ya'll ain't scared," laughed K.C.

"Nah Shorty, ain't nobody scared over here. We just over here talking business, you know. A'ight love, nothing personal." Ness turned to face her while Smitty kept his back towards her.

"A'ight! Well come on Keish, let's not keep the boys from discussing man shit. Later, K.C." Epiphany grabbed Keisha's arm and began to pull her away.

"Okay, take care K.C." Keisha said as she was being whisk away.

"You see, that's exactly why I couldn't fuck with that bitch. That mouth of hers is off the chain." Smitty fronted to his boys like it was his choice and not his actions that caused her not to fuck with him.

"Girl, why you do that? That guy was kinda cute." Keisha said referring to Ness.

"Please, no he wasn't. Girl, I got to teach you how to separate the fakes from the real ballers. That was a fake one." Epiphany said rolling her eyes.

"Ooh, come on E there's the camera man. Let's go take a picture." Keisha screamed.

"Whew! Look at you pretty ladies," said the camera man as he snapped several pictures of the girls. "Okay ladies," he continued, "log on to allnightclubs.com tomorrow afternoon and look for your photos."

"Oh, so they're gonna be online?" asked Epiphany.

"Yes ma'am, every picture I take is posted at that website," answered the camera man.

"Cool." replied Keisha.

"Come on Keish, ain't nothing really happening in here, let's bounce." Epiphany said as she sucked her teeth to express her disappointment with the club's crowd.

On the way out they spotted K.C. in the corner kissing some hood rat looking bitch.

"Hold-up E, ain't that K.C. over there, all on that girl like that?" asked Keisha.

"Oooooh, yes the fuck it is." Epiphany confirmed.

"Uh un, I'm going over to say something," said Keisha.

"No, don't. I got a better idea. Wait right here." Epiphany walked back over to the photographer. "Excuse me how good is the zoom on your camera."

"It's excellent, why?" Answered the camera man.

"I got fifty bucks for you, if you could zoom in on the guy over there in the corner with that girl and snap a picture for me, but you got to put it on the web."

"No problem," agreed the camera man as he took the crisp fifty dollar bill and slide it into his side pocket, zoomed in on the target and snapped a perfect shot.

"Thanks." Epiphany said as she walked back towards Keisha wearing a devious grin.

"Damn E, you still scandalous," laughed Keisha.

"Yep! A picture *is* worth a thousand words." The girls left the club and headed home. Fortunately for them the night turned out to be eventful, after all.

CHAPTER 26

"Please don't hurt me," Epiphany cried out as she laid balled up in a fetal position trying to shield herself from the kicks and punches that were landing one after another bruising and paining her body. Suddenly, it stopped, but Epiphany was too scared to hold up her head to see what was going on.

"Damn son, you fucking that hoe up." An unrecognizable male's voice laughed. More then one person was present. There was a moment of silence and just as Epiphany begin to slightly lift her head to see what was going on and who was doing it, the telephone rang waking her from the horrible nightmare. She rolled over on her back, relieved that it was all just a bad dream, or was it she thought.

"Keisha answer your phone." Epiphany realized she was in Keisha's guest bedroom. "Damn it. Hello?" Epiphany grabbed the receiver with an irritated tone.

"Yeah, what took you so long to answer the phone?" Tucker asked.

"What, who is this?" Epiphany snapped, not realizing that it could only be Tucker calling.

"*Who is this?*" Tucker snapped back.

"Listen, you called here therefore you need to announce yourself or I'm hanging up."

"Bitch, that's my phone you answering, now get my son's mother on the phone." Tucker said angrily.

"Oops! Sorry Tucker, I didn't know it was you. This is Epiphany," she said not knowing that she just added fuel to Tucker's fire. He despised her.

"Yeah, yeah, yeah just call Keish to the phone."

"Hey T, I know you're sore about what happen to Mali, but your not the only one feeling the pain of his death, you know."

"Call Keish to the fucking phone, PLEASE."

"I already tried that before I picked up, so obviously she ain't here and hopefully I won't forget to let her know you called. Bye, now." Epiphany grew furious from his response and hung up the phone. Getting up, she headed to Keisha's bedroom. Since the door was slightly opened, Epiphany peaked in before entering.

"Keisha, wake up. Get up girl," Epiphany said loudly as she plopped down on what use to be Tucker's side of the bed.

"What?" replied Keisha, frowning up her face when the scent of her morning breath mixed with last night's alcohol hit her nose.

"Tucker just called for you."

"He did, what did he say?"

"Well first off, he wasn't to thrilled with me answering his phone." Epiphany admitted.

"Why, what did you say?" asked Keisha.

"I was trying to be nice, but he was the one acting all nasty, so I told him you wasn't here."

"Girl it's eight o'clock in the morning, you know what he gon' think," said Keisha.

"And, so what? Let him think it. I'm telling you, if you start acting like you moved on, trust me, he'll be back."

"You think so?"

"Yes I do, trust me when I tell you. If I don't know nothing else, I know niggas. I'm telling you, I could write a book on they're asses. They may come in all shapes, sizes and colors, but they all think the same. Girl, please believe me." If there was one thing that Epiphany didn't lose, it was her confidence. "Seriously Keish, does Tucker think I killed Malikai?"

"No, but he does think that maybe you had something to do with it," answered Keisha.

"And what do you think, Keisha?"

"Come on girl, me and you go way back like Pimps and Cadillac's." Keisha laughed, covering her mouth with her sheets.

"I know that, but you still ain't answer the question." Epiphany continued.

"No Epiphany, I don't think you had anything to do with Malikai getting murdered." Keisha stopped laughing. She realized that her friend was really worried.

"Good, because even though I don't remember what happened, I know in my heart I didn't have anything to do with that." Tears began to puddle up in her eyes.

"I know and that's exactly what I told T, so don't even worry about it girl. He's just bitter right now, because he wasn't able to save Mali, that's all." Keisha sat up and put her arm around Epiphany.

"Before the phone woke me up, I was having this terrible dream, but I don't think it was just a dream. I think maybe it really happened.

"What was it about?"

111

"I really don't want to get into details right now, but just as I was about to see their faces, the phone rang and I woke up.

"Do you think your memory is trying to come back?"

"I don't know, but I hope so," said Epiphany just as the phone rang again breaking her train of thought. "You better answer it this time, 'cause I'm sure it's Tucker calling you back," smiled Epiphany as she got up to leave the room.

"Hello?" Keisha answered.

"What's up girly?" said the cheery voice on the other end of the line.

"Um, who is this?"

"It's Lea girl!"

"Oh hey Lea, ain't heard from you in a while."

"I know, girl I've been so tied up with finals and all that, but I've been meaning to call you for a while now. Why haven't you been to class? You busy planning that wedding of yours?"

"No, the wedding is off," answered Keisha.

"Why, what's up with that? You guys are still going to get married, right?" Lea questioned.

"Lea, don't act like you don't know about the tape."

"What tape?"

"Come on Lea, don't you think it's a little ironic that you begged me to have that party and those strippers. *"Oh come on Keisha, you can go to the club anytime. This might be the last time you see some dicks slinging in your face."* Remember that? Then all of a sudden a video tape from that night shows up on my fucking door step." Keisha's voice was getting louder.

"Keisha, I can't believe that you would think that I would do something like that." Lea was taken back by Keisha's accusation.

"Okay, so if you didn't set me up, why haven't you called me until now?"

"I told you why-school. Besides, Simone told me she spoke to you and things were cool with you."

"Whatever Lea, school has never stopped you from calling me before."

"Keisha, If you really wanna get technical, most of our conversations took place in school. I never really called you at home in the first place, except for once or twice to talk about your wedding. But you know what, it's sad that out of everybody there that night you would accuse me. What about the other girls? Simone, helped me put the whole thing together. Or how about the girl that came with you? What about your friend, Epiphany? She was the last one to leave the room.

"Well Epiphany wouldn't do that to me, neither would Shana and Simone. Come on, she doesn't even seem like the type that would something like that."

"Oh, and I would?"

"Well at first I didn't think you would, but the room was in your name therefore you had time to set up a camcorder before anybody got there."

"Oh, is that right? Well you know what Keisha, I 'm not going to sit here and try to defend myself any longer. If you think I did it, fine. But I certainly didn't forced you in the other room and make you have sex with that guy, now did I?" Keisha was speechless. "Yeah, that's what I thought," Lea said sarcastically before hanging up the phone. If that wasn't enough drama for one morning, soon after she hung up with Lea, Tucker came barging into her bedroom.

"Keish, what the fuck is that bitch doing in my house, huh? What is it with you? You think I'm that nigga don't you—that's what it is, huh? Just some muthafucka that you could all run over, right? I guess 'cause I ain't knock some sense into you yet.

Are you testing me? Fuck me, right? You ain't got no fucking respect for me, do you?"

"What are you talking about?" Keisha said playing the stupid role, when she knew exactly why he was upset. That only made Tucker more furious, so furious that he snapped and slapped the shit out of her. She let out a horrifying cry. Tucker had never put his hands on her before nor did she ever expect him to.

"Yeah you know what I'm talking about now, don't you? Where the fuck is my son at, huh? He was suppose to come home yesterday. I called your moms and she told me some bogus bullshit about you needing two more weeks. Two more weeks for what, Keisha? To hop your ass in and out the clubs? Yeah, I heard. So, that's what you wanna do, huh, club hop?"

Still stunned from being slapped, Keisha didn't answer. Her face was beginning to swell. She sat there massaging her cheek with one hand, soothing the stinging and wiped her tears away as with the other hand.

"All you do is cry Keisha. I don't care about those fucking tears of yours. I've been trying to be cool throughout everything, but no, you stay pushing my fucking buttons. Damn Keish, how much is a nigga suppose to take from you?" Tucker was fed up with Keisha's bull and in his heart he was beginning to feel like she really had no respect for him anymore. She didn't appreciate him, or nothing he did for her. So as far as he was concerned it was time to let her go, move on and put an end to the 'Tucker and Keisha" chapter of his life for good.

"Keish, you got to go!" Tucker realized that was the best and only decision to make.

"What...what do you mean?"

"I mean, I'm not taking care of you no more. My son is my responsibility–not you."

"Wait a minute, my name is on this house, too. How you just gon' put me out like that, T? I'm your son's mother, where are we suppose to go?" Keisha pleaded.

"Keisha, I told you before, I'm not trying to hear all that. This is my house, I pay all the bills. Your name don't mean shit, so stop it. It's not gonna fly and if you feel differently take me to court. Okay! Now, yes, you are my son's mother and I will take care of all my little man's needs—there's no questions about that, but you got two more weeks to yourself. I suggest you spend them looking for a place to stay."

Keisha wasn't gonna fight it anymore. Time and time again, Tucker made it clear that it was over between them. She packed some of her things and as she was about to leave he asked for her keys. She removed them slowly from her key chain and threw them on the bed.

"Hold up, I'ma need the keys to the truck too," he added, taking it to the extreme. Keisha cut her eyes at him. *'I hate you'* she thought as she tossed the whole key chain onto the bed and stormed off.

"Thank you." Tucker said sarcastically.

Meanwhile, just when Tucker asked Keisha for the keys, Epiphany felt her ears had heard enough. She eased down the stairs, grabbed her bags and decided it would be best if she sat outside in her car and waited for Keisha. She didn't wanna be the next one to get slapped.

Triple Crown Publications presents

CHAPTER 27

C-God was slowly fading away; getting high whenever he could. Money was starting to get tight. Marisa lost her job at the grocery store and made her bills become his problem. C-God wasn't supplying her with any more coke, so she jumped on the band wagon and started sucking on the glass pipe with him. In Marisa's mind it was only for a little while—just until she lost some weight—but if only she knew, dropping the weight would be the easy part. The addiction had a hell of a price to pay and her children were the first to suffer. Why, because getting high became more important to her then their needs. Most of the time she stayed locked up in her bedroom for hours with C-God smoking crack, while the kids knocks for food, help with the homework or just some quality time went ignored. Her children hated C-god and blamed him for their mother's neglect.

Reggie still communicated with C-God from time to time, to see how he was doing. Although he chose to roll with Ness for money purposes, he still had love for the nigga C. C-God understood that it wasn't about him. He knew Reggie had a lot on his plate—trying to take care of his grandmother, who he loved dearly and hustled daily, through rain, sleet and snow to get up the doe to take care of her bills and live in nurse. Reg kept C-god informed about what was going on and the moves niggas was making in the hood. He was the eyes and ears on the street that C-God no longer had, his information was priceless. C-God was surprised when Reg called and told him how his baby moms Latrice went out.

"Yo son, they played Latrice?" said Reggie.

"Who?"

"That nigga Ness, man. Out in front of the projects the other day, he had her sucking on a dog's dick for that crack. Shit, in front of everybody too, just 'cause she was short a dollar. Yo C, I tried to stop her, but she wanted them drugs bad." C- God was quite. He flashed back to how fly Latrice use to be and that smart mouth of her's. All the ballers tried to get at her back in the day, but she chose C-God when he ain't have a pot to piss in or a window to throw it out of and he love her for that. That is until he started getting money and the golddiggers took notice. His excuse for moving on to the next chick was Latrice's jealousy and crazed antics after giving birth to their first child. Reminiscing made C-God think about all his baby momma's. To let him tell it, all of them where some bugged out bitches. Latrice and Sherri had lost custody of his kids, Lori and Jasmine, because of their crack addictions. Andrea married some Wall Street cat, who adopted C-God's seven-year old daughter, Atria, and moved them out to the Hamptons. Kim has a good paying city job, but stay trying to hit him up for money for their son Corey, who's seven also. Then Yolonda's weed smoking, welfare collecting ass, did nothing but get her fuck on with different niggas and threatened C with child support orders every chance she got. Sad to say, out of all of them, she was the one that had C-God open. He made her his wifey, before finding out how who-rish she really was and until this day he still questions if he's the father of her daughters, Kameechie and Yaya. Last, but not least, there's Tanya. She's a good girl— smart and educated, C-god never had no problems with her. She's still young, so she does what she's told and she has a strong supportive family and they all take care good of his son.

"Yo C, you there?" Reggie wasn't certain C was still on the phone. He had been silent for a minute.

"Yeah, I'm here. Anyway fuck Latrice, Tanya's the only one out all them bitches that I give a fuck about. That's why I need you to check up on her from time to time and make sure she's good, a'ight? Do that for me until I get on my feet."

"Not a problem." Reggie said.

"Oh and one more thing, any word on Epiphany, you know the chick I was fucking with?" C-God asked.

"Yeah, I know who you talking about. I hear she a'ight, as a matter of fact, her pops came through the projects a couple of times looking for you."

"Word? I know what that's about, but it wasn't me. I'm glad she a'ight though. Anyway thanks, good looking out fam."

"It's nothing, I'ma holla at you later, a'ight?" said Reg.

"A'ight man."

Triple Crown Publications presents

CHAPTER 28

Shana was so upset after Epiphany and Keisha called to tell her about K.C.'s behavior at the club the other night. Keisha had the proof but didn't have access to a computer in order to print it out.

"What's wrong with your computer, Keish?" Shana questioned.

"Nothing, I'm staying with Epiphany for a while," answered Keisha.

"Shana, you can use my computer as soon as my pops gets my stuff out of storage." Epiphany offered.

"And when is that?"

"Probably next week, once he's done fixing up the basement for me and Keisha." Epiphany answered.

"Shit, I can't wait that long."

"So, what you gonna do, huh, tell him we told you?" asked Epiphany.

"I don't know what I'm gonna do, but I know I ain't gon' be able to hold this shit in for a week," replied Shana.

"See that's some bullshit. We look out for you and you gonna tell the nigga. If it was meant to go down like that, I wouldn't have paid the camera man fifty dollars." Epiphany complained.

"Yo, I'll give you your fifty dollars back, that's not a problem." Shana said.

"You're right, the money ain't the problem, it's your fucking mouth," said Epiphany.

"Fuck you Epiphany, don't tell me shit next time," yelled Shana.

"Fuck you, too. I won't, believe that."

"Come on you guys this ain't necessary and Shana, Epiphany is right this time. It ain't cool for you to rat us out like that and have your man hating on us." Keisha explained.

"So what I'm I supposed to do, go out and buy a computer just so I can confront his ass." Shana said sarcastically.

"No, we can go to Kinko's and use their internet access." Keisha suggested.

"That'll work, but why didn't you suggest that in the first place?" Shana asked.

"Because, I just thought about it while you and Epiphany were going at it. Now can you two apologize please?" said Keisha.

"I'm sorry E," Shana said nonchalantly.

"Whatever, just get me my fifty bucks," said Epiphany still wanting to hold a grudge.

"Yo Keish, you see what I mean, fuck that bitc-" Before she could finish , Keisha took the phone off speaker and picked up the receiver while Shana continued to express how she felt about Epiphany.

"Shana, just come and get me alright; I don't have my car," said Keisha changing the subject and calming down Shana.

"A'ight, I'm on my way," said Shana.

When Shana arrived, she called Keisha on her cell to let her know she was out front.

"Hey E, I'll be back, Shana's out front." Keisha said.

"Yeah a'ight, get my money from that bitch please." Epiphany replied.

"Uh huh." Keisha walked out shaking her head not able to understand, why the two of them just couldn't get along.

Once Keisha left, Epiphany went outside and sat on the stoop of her parents' house, which was something she hadn't done since she was a kid. It had to be about 90 degrees out, the sun was blazing. As she watched the kids on the corner running in and out of the fire hydrant, laughing, playing and having a good time, while trying to stay cool, she remembered some things. This time, it was clear. She could recall taking a home pregnancy test and it being positive, the pain she felt from all his kicks and punches, but most importantly she could remember his face. *"It was C-God,"* she mumbled as her memory confirmed her father and Keisha's beliefs. Epiphany felt awful, it just didn't make sense to her at all and there was still a lot of information missing. *'Why did he try to kill me'* she though. *'Was it because I found out I was pregnant or maybe it was Mali's baby, but, no, Keisha said I stopped seeing Malikai months ago. So maybe I wasn't really-'* The ring of her cell phone broke her heavy train of thought. It was someone calling from a 323 area code.

'323 where the fuck is that?' "Hello?" Epiphany answered.

"What up, Beautiful?" said the man's voice.

"You got the beautiful part right, but who is this?" She responded.

"Damn Ma, you forgot about me already, huh? It's Wild, how you doing?"

"Oh hey, I'm good. I thought you forgot about me."

"Nah never that, I just been tied up out here in LA trying to blaze some tracks, that's all."

"Oh, so when you coming back to NY?"

"I'm flying in tonight, late night, but I was hoping we can get together sometime tomorrow.

"Well, call me tomorrow and I'll let you know." Epiphany didn't want to seem as anxious as she really was.

"Oh, you'll let me know, huh? Why you can't just say yeah now?"

"Because, I'm gonna be kind of busy tomorrow. I don't wanna commit to anything now and then have to disappoint you later. You know what I'm saying? It's called having considera-tion." Epiphany said with sarcasm.

"I'll see you tomorrow, early, so we could spend all day and night together, a'ight shorty?" Wild disregarded her weak excuse. His confidence turned her on and brought a smile to her face.

"Yeah okay, I'll see you tomorrow. Bye" Wild's call had com-pletely taken her mind off of her revelations, well maybe not completely, but Epiphany was starting to feel like the more she remembered about her past and it's horrid details the less she wanted to remember. *'Maybe it was best to just put it all behind me, besides no one has seen or heard from C- God anyway.'*

CHAPTER 29

Once Shana dropped Keisha back off at Epiphany's parents house she went home and waited impatiently for K.C. to get his ass home. She sat on the couch staring at the glossy Kodak print out of him all over some high yellow bitch, who looked like she might have been cute if she didn't suffered from a severe case of ache. She was ticked off, but the funny thing about the whole situation was that she already had a gut feeling that he was fucking around on her. If that wasn't enough evidence, her suffering from dick deprivation should have been another clue. It seems like the only time he wanted to fuck her was when she wanted to argue about his bullshit behavior. Shana wasn't happy. K.C. was obviously doing him, the bitch in the photo and who ever else he was out there screwing, but it certainly wasn't her.

'I can't believe I'm still paying that muthafucka, Smitty, money, for what? To keep a dumb little secret from a nigga that don't even want to be kept.' Just as that thought ran through Shana's mind she heard K.C.'s keys rattling at the door. Quickly, she laid the photo down right in front of her, on the coffee table, just to see how long it would take him to notice it. Only, when he walked in he wasn't alone, Smitty trailed in right behind him. Instantly, her attitude got worst, sucking her teeth she snatch up the picture not wanting Smitty all up in their business, although he most likely knew way more dirt then she could ever imagine.

"What up, Sha?" K.C. said as he placed his car keys and cell phone down on the coffee table, right in the same spot the photo was.

"I need to talk to you, but I see you got your shadow with you." Shana said giving K.C. the head movement and eye rolling treatment.

"Well hello to you to, Sha." Smitty said to further aggravate her. Shana just rolled her eyes again and waited for K.C.'s response.

"Yeah, so can't it wait?" K.C. said.

"No it can't fucking wait, I'm tired of being put on hold for this muthafucka," she said pointing at Smitty. "So either you excuse him, or I'll say what the fuck I gotta say right in front of him."

"Yo Smitty, you see what the fuck I gotta deal with all the time. Yo, I'm telling you, a nigga be trying to keep from fucking a bitch up." K.C. said feeling like Shana was trying to punk him in front of his boy. His nose began to flare up and he balled his fist tightly trying to compose his anger.

"Yeah nigga I, feel you, but yo I'm out. You need to get that shit under wraps dawg, cause word up she stay with an attitude." Smitty added his two cents, as usual.

"I'ma handle this, but just hit me later." K.C. said.

"Who the fuck is this bitch, huh?" Shana raised her voice as soon as he shut the door behind Smitty. Waiving the photo in K.C. face she demanded an answer. "Yeah, muthafucka you busted." K.C. looked closely at the picture and laughed.

"Where you get that from? I don't know who she is and that ain't me."

"You'se a lying ass. So, that's how you gon' go out, huh? You can't even be a man and admit the shit you do. Who is she, K.C.?"

"Yo, I'm out man, because you be bugging the fuck out and I'm telling you, you gon' make me fuck you up." K.C. reached for his car keys on the table. Shana made a quick dash for the keys along with his cell phone and hauled ass to the bedroom locking the door behind her.

"Now muthafucka you wanna play games? Lets play games. You ain't going no-fucking-where. I got your phone and your key, so if you want your shit back you better start confessing nigga." Shana yelled from the other side of the door while trying to catch her breath from that olympic sprint she just made.

"Bitch don't fuck with me, open the door and give me my shit." K.C. shouted as he tried to kick down the door. Yo wait 'til I open this door, Shana. I'm a-" K.C. had to catch his breath. "Yo, I think you be wanting a nigga to fuck you up—you like that shit, huh? Open this fucking door!!!" Shana ignored his threats and continued to question the girl's identity while he stood on the other side of the bedroom door, trying to figure out a way to pick the lock or bust through it. Inside she prayed hard that the door would not give –way.

"Let me see, Kiana. Who the fuck is Kiana? Latrell, Meeka, Valerie," Shana called out each females name as she strolled down and deleted them out of his phones memory, one by one. "Just tell me who this chick in the picture is. I see you've been real busy lately, but where was all these hoes at when your ass was locked up, huh? I can't do this shit no more K.C." Shana screamed.

"Ahhh, come on Sha." K.C. showed a little compassion for her feelings. "Listen Sha, them bitches don't mean shit to me, a'ight. I'll admit, occasionally I *might* fuck around on you, but that shit don't mean that I don't love you. You just need to understand that I was married to this drug game shit, the streets and every thing in it, long before you and on the real those are the only things I know how to be committed to. The streets ain't never going nowhere and cause of that, a nigga like me gon' always get paper."

"K.C., what does all of that have to do with you fucking around on me?"

"Sha, didn't I just say, I don't give a fuck about those bitches. They just hoes that come alone with the game. I made you my wife, but you need to accept me for the nigga I am and the fucked up shit I do, because at the end of the day I'm coming home to you. Yeah I fucked up the other night, but I was out all night handling business. Sha you held me down when I was fucked up, so I ain't gon' never play you. Now open the door."

"K.C. I'm not gonna open the door until you tell me who this girl is."

"Yo, are you hearing what I said to you? She ain't nobody Sha, so stop dwelling on that hoe and open the door. Come on yo, I ain't gonna do nothing to you. I just wanna chill with you, a'ight, open the door."

Shana unlocked the door and slowly backed away from it just incase he came in swinging. Fortunately for Shana, K.C. had already gotten over being mad thirty minutes ago, besides the number one rule in the players manual is to always treat the one you love better than the hoes you fuck. He knew in order to keep the peace, you had to take care of home first and he wasn't holding down that part. So for the rest of the evening he did some serious making up in hopes that Shana would get off his back for a while.

CHAPTER 30

"Yo, how I get to you?" Wild said as soon a Epiphany picked up her cellphone.

"Well, hello to you, too." Epiphany said as she glanced over at the clock, which read 9:00 am.

"Oh my bad, hello pretty, now how do I get to you once I hit Queens?" Epiphany smiled, liking his persistence, and gave him directions. "A'ight, I should be there in like 45 minutes and bring a few things just in case I decide to kidnap you for a couple of days."

"Okay, I'll see you when you get here." After ending the call, Epiphany excitedly jumped out of bed to search through her many clothes for the right outfits to pack. She decided to wear her hot pink Roberto Cavalli sundress along with her Prada sandals and matching purse. She packed three other cute outfits that showed expensive taste, class and style, because by no means did she want him to think she was anything less than fabulous. Keisha was awakened by the noise Epiphany made as she rush to get herself together.

"Girl, where you going?" she asked.

"Oh, remember the guy that I was chilling with at Suede, the producer I told you about?"

"Yeah." Keisha said.

"Well, I'll be with him for a couple of days." answered Epiphany.

"I hear that, have fun. I got me a date tonight, too," boasted Keisha.

"Get out, you mean to tell me that you finally decide to move on. With who?"

"With this guy I met at Kinko's yesterday with Shana."

"He works in Kinko's?" Epiphany said, not even trying to hide her disgust.

"No, he repairs computers for Kinko's. Anyway, I don't care where he works, just as long as he works because I think I'm done with drug dealers."

"I hear that, to each his own. Anyway, what's his name?"

"His name is Rob, he's a cutie."

"Well good for you Keish, you need to get out and have some fun, make sure that nigga spends his pay check. Let me go shower before Wild gets here." Epiphany was happy for her friend but abruptly ending their conversation, running to the bathroom to freshen up.

Wild pulled in front of Epiphany's parent's crib and phoned her to come outside. When she reached the front door she fell in love with his sparkling silver Hummer, not the affordable h2 Hummer—this was the real deal.

"What's up sexy, don't I get a kiss," asked Wild as he held the car door open for.

"Nah, I don't kiss on the first date." laughed Epiphany.

"I respect that."

"Good." Epiphany played it cool, but in her mind she was screaming *'Fuck a kiss, I'm gonna fuck the shit out of this nigga.'*

Once they crossed over the George Washington bridge heading towards Route 4, Wild phoned his cook and told him to start preparing breakfast for two.

"You like omelets?" he asked.

"Yeah, they're alright!" Epiphany answered.

"Well my chef Idris makes some banging ass omelets, you'll love em." Twenty minutes later, they pulled up to a tall black gate that Wild opened with a little remote like gadget. Epiphany was still trying to get over the fact that he had a chef when he pulled into a four car garage next to a convertible black Bentley. *'This is so beautiful,'* she thought as she looked around the grounds, while he got out of the driver's side and rush over to open the car door for her again. He was being the perfect gentlemen. His 2.5 million, eight-bedroom house was located in the ultra chic Englewood Cliffs, New Jersey and came equipped with an outdoor in-ground swimming poor, sauna, a huge patio and a basketball court. Indoors was a gym, a small movie theater, a recording studio and a game room. Epiphany had to admit that this was far more impressive then any nice car or house she'd ever seen in her life. This was the type of lifestyle she felt she was born to live, she was tired of dealing with the small time hustlers in the hood, who were satisfied with the minimum— a little bit of jewelry, a hot ride, at least fifty-grand stashed in an old sneaker box and a laced-out apartment in the projects, thinking life is sweet. She wanted to live like a celebrity and if she played her cards right, Mr. Producer Man could be her ticket out of the ghetto. He escorted her straight to the kitchen for the best breakfast she had ever had. After breakfast, Wild gave Epiphany a personal tour. *'This house is defiantly made for MTV's cribs'* she thought as they entered the master bedroom. It had a brick fireplace, a king size bed with plush feathered pillows and a matching cream colored comforter. The bathroom was all marble with an oval-shaped Jacuzzi and attached shower. His walk in closet was bigger than the bedroom in Epiphany's old apartment and being the fashion fanatic that she was she couldn't help but to take a look in inside. According to her, you can tell a lot about a person from his or her style of dress. One side of his closet had at least two-hundred pairs of jeans and button up shirts from every designer neatly hanging up, stacks of starter hats on the shelves, velour sweat suits, about fifty pairs of white on white air force ones, five pairs of Jordans, a couple of S. Carter's and too many pairs of Timbs to count. Epiphany could tell judging by the amount of suits and shoes he owned that he wasn't big on dressing up, but when he did at least he did his thing by rocking designer names like Armani, Salvatore Ferragamo, Ralph Lauren, and Gucci. Last but not least, she glided her hands up and down his mink jackets and butter soft *Iso Life* leathers. She couldn't help but hum the tune *Why don't we fall in love* by Amerie. Why not? He had everything she wanted.

CHAPTER 31

Ness, Smitty and K.C. were doing the damn thing, making money in the hood. Since other niggas had no real weight in the streets, it was easy. But lately, problems were occurring in their own circle. Smitty started to feel like Ness was getting besides himself, on some real control shit. He kept quiet for a minute, letting the nigga run wild with it, and assumed that maybe it was just a power trip. Ness had never been in a position to call the shots. Smitty decided to let him have his fun before he'd pump his brakes. Only, Ness was on some Nino Brown type shit. All of a sudden the streets were his; he made all the decisions, gave the orders, handled most of the money and was reckless with his mouth and his decisions. Now, a real trouble maker, he created unnecessary drama with this kid named Righteous from Lefrak City. Ness had an altercation with him at a traffic light one day, 'cause he felt dude disrespected him by cutting in front of him without using his signal. The truth was, Righteous had shit locked down on his side of Queens— selling top quality cocaine for fifty bucks a pop. The coke heads loved him and the crack heads preferred to buy his shit and cook it up themselves because they got more for their money. Word was spreading around Queens about dude's product and price and Ness wasn't happy about that. He ain't want nobody getting money in Southside, Jamaica, but him. Eventually, Righteous would be a problem. Ness arranged to meet up with Smitty and K.C. in Ajax park to discuss how they should handle their competition. When

Smitty and K.C. arrived, Ness was on the empty court with his shirt off shooting hoops.

"Yo, what up my niggas?" Ness greeted them with a pound.

"Ain't shit." Smitty responded.

"Chilling," answered K.C.

"Yo Smitt, how's shit moving over there by you?" Ness asked.

"Yo son, shits been a'ight, why? What up?"

"Word, what about by you, K?" Ness questioned.

"Everything's straight where I'm at dawg." K.C. answered.

"Yo what's up with that kid Righteous, ya'll heard of that nigga?" Ness was still shooting around.

"Yeah, I met dude when I was up north, he's a cool nigga." K.C. said.

"Um, what he do time for?" Ness inquired.

"He caught a one-to-three for some bullshit." K.C.

"Well, that nigga should've stayed locked the fuck up, 'cause I don't like him."

"Come on man, ain't no need to get caught up in no bullshit over some nonsense. We don't need that type of heat right now," said Smitty.

"Smitt, man, what's up with you? You been on some real sucker shit lately.

"Cause man, you be on some bullshit. You getting real loose with the words, 'I' and 'my'. This shit ain't yours alone nigga. You need to leave all that unnecessary drama alone and try to stay focused on what we doing dawg." Smitty couldn't believe that Ness was coming at them like that.

"Unnecessary drama, what the fuck you talking about? That muthafucka just came home and already he trying to interfere with *my* fucking money. Shit ain't going down like that. I ain't gon' let a muthafucka move in on me. Just like I did with that nigga C, niggas gon' know that I ain't that dude. I'ma make an example out of any nigga that tries to step up." Ness sounded like a mad man.

"Yo dawg, just leave that shit alone?" K.C. just wanted to drop it already.

"Quite naturally you gon' say that. Nigga, you just fucking stood here and said you was cool with dude, so I ain't even fucking with you right now!"

"Yo, me and that nigga ain't tight. I ain't say I'll break bread with 'em. You're bugging. I could see if that nigga, Righteous, was trying to get at you, but you hating on the man for trying to eat. What he got going ain't even putting no dents our pockets dawg!" K.C. responded.

"Well I still ain't feeling kid, yo, and I ain't gonna wait until he become a problem. You'se Smitty's man, dawg, so why is you even talking to me anyway, huh?" K.C. didn't feed into Ness's cocky ass bullshit, he just shook his head thinking to himself *'this nigga done really bugged the fuck out.'*

"Yo, I'm out." Ness said throwing his shirt back on as he headed towards his Range Rover. *'Fuck ya'll pussy ass niggas'* he mumbled, hopping inside his truck. He sat there for a moment, sparked up some haze, then pumped up the sounds of B.I.G.'s *'What's beef'*and skid off like a maniac. Everything Smitty and K.C had said went in one ear and out the other, as he bopped his head to the lyrics. *'Beef is when you make ya enemies start ya jeep, beef is when you roll no less then thirty deep, beef is when I see you guaranteed to be in ICU...'*

The high from the purple haze made him feel like the baddest nigga alive with murder on the brain. He turned down his radio and slowly crept down the streets of Lefrak housing approaching the area were Righteous usually hung out at. Ness didn't really know the niggas description, as far as his height and weight. Their beef took place while they both were driving and he vaguely remembered his facial features, but that wasn't going to stop his plans. He parked his truck and waited.

"Yo shorty c'mere" Ness called out to a young boy around sixteen, as he walked past. Ness noticed the kid's hesitation. "C'mere, I ain't gon' do shit to you. For real, I just wanna ask you something."

Not sure whether or not he could trust Ness's word, the boy slowly walked over towards the truck, his palms started to sweat and his heart pounded rapidly.

"Yo, lil' man you scared, I told you I ain't gon' fuck with you. I just want you to do something for me, a'ight?" said Ness. The boy slowly shook his head 'yes'.

"You talk, little nigga?" Ness asked sarcastically.

This time the boy answered, "Yeah."

"A'ight, good, that's better! Yo, you know Righteous?"

The boy shook his head 'yes' instead of opening his mouth, making Ness so angry he stared to yell at the kid.

"Yo man, I thought you said you could fucking talk?"

"I c-can," stuttered the frightened boy.

"Then answer me nigga and stop shaking your fucking head, now yes or no do you know him?"

"Uh huh."

"Is he out here, right now?"

"Yeah."

"A'ight then, without pointing, where?"

"He across the street in front of the bodega on the corner."

"A'ight what he got on?" Ness asked.

"I think he got on a green and white shirt and some jeans ," said the boy.

"You think, or you sure?"

"I'm sure." answered the boy.

"A'ight, good lookin' out. Here," Ness handed the boy five twenty-dollar bills and left him with words of advice, "Toughen up shorty, learn how to open your fucking mouth and speak, a'ight!"

The boy didn't answer he just clutched onto the bills tightly and took off running wanting no part of any mess that Ness was up to. Slowly, Ness drove up to the bodega and sure enough he spotted Righteous wearing a green a white Celtics jersey, standing in front of the store hugged up on some chick. Ness got out of his truck and walked up on him.

"Yo, what up nigga?"

"What up? I know you, dawg?" Righteous slightly pushed his girl to the side. It didn't dawn on him that Ness was the guy from the traffic light. That was some minor bullshit he brushed off, but Ness didn't look at it that way."

"Nah son, you don't know me, but we bumped heads a few days ago. I came to tell you that you can't pump that shit you selling around here no more." "What, who the fuck is you, dawg? This me over here nigga, I own Lefrak. I gotta give it to you, you a bold ass bastard." Righteous was taking Ness for some little clown ass nigga.

"Oh word, I'm funny, huh?" Ness quickly pulled out his .38 and unloaded four bullets into dude's chest. Since their conversation never got loud, no one anticipated any kind of beef so when the shots rang the few cats that was around scattered, instead of coming to Righteous' defense.

"Yeah nigga. I'll be funny, but how bout that was your last laugh." said Ness, calmly he pointing his smoking gun at the frantically crying girl who was with Righteous. "Shut the fuck up bitch," He silenced her with one to the head and hopped back in his truck speeding off.

CHAPTER 32

Keisha kept watching the clock anticipating her date with Rob. It seemed like time moved extra slow just because she looked forward to finally moving on. It had been almost two weeks since Tucker kicked her out and he hadn't even tried to contact her yet. However, he managed to call Loretta at least two times a day to check up on their son. Keisha started to get jealous when Loretta would say *'he called'*, so her calls slowly started to decrease. She hated the fact that Tucker cared about their son more then he cared about her, when for seven years she was his number one, now she felt invisible. It wasn't that she didn't love her son, because she did with all her heart, but she felt the three of them were *supposed* to be a family. Keisha wanted a reason to hate Tucker, she started to blame him for what she felt she missed out on—*her teenage years*. That didn't work. Regardless of how bad she tried to paint the picture she couldn't ignore the fact that Tucker never put restrictions on her and was only guilty of taking care of her and providing a comfortable life for the both of them. She had a good man and hated herself more and more for cheating. Out of spite, Keisha felt it would be best if her son stayed in Atlanta with her mother. *'If Tucker can't find it in his heart to forgive me, so we could raised our son together, then he'll never see him again.'*

Rob was in front of the house beeping his horn at exactly eight o'clock on the dot. Mrs. Wright rushed over to the window to see who was in front of her house blowing their horn *'like a darn fool,'* when Keisha came running towards the door.

"Is that for you Keisha?" she asked.

"Yeah, I think so."

"I should hope not 'cause a real man would get out the car and ring the bell." Mrs. Wright said.

"I'm sorry Mrs. T, maybe he isn't sure which house to come to." Keisha said as she went out the door.

"Hey, Rob." Keisha was wearing a big smile once she got in his car.

"What's up, baby?" he responded.

She giggled and then answered "Nothing."

"So, where you wanna go?"

"Wherever you wanna go?"

"Well, I was thinking we could make this a blockbuster night."

"Blockbuster night, huh? Well I haven't been out in a long time so what kind of date is that?" she asked.

"That's you, me, and a movie from blockbuster at my crib."

'That ain't no real date', she thought, but if his company could help take her mind off Tucker then why not. "Okay" she replied. Rob's studio apartment looked like a real bachelor's pad—no sense of style, everything was black or gray and he did-n't appear to be a neat person. Especially, since he had to push a pile of dirty clothes off the bed for Keisha to have a seat.

"Okay, which movie do you want to see, *The Italian Job* or *Unfaithful*?" There was no way Keisha was gonna sit and watch a movie about a woman *cheating* on her man so she selected *The Italian Job*. Rob popped in the DVD, pressed play and before the previews could finish he was all over Keisha. He started to kissed on her neck as he ran his hand slowly between her closed thighs. Keisha let out a soft moan and slightly opened her legs, giving him the okay to continue. Rob climbed on top of her and started to rubbed the erection that bulged from his jeans up against her as their tongues intertwined. Winding her hips in circular motions, Keisha's moans got louder as her panties started to get wet. Rob unfastened her bra and encircled her perky B cups into his hand as he softly sucked and gently bit her nipples.

"Oooh yes," she moaned as her pussy throbbed for his dick. Rob raised up for a moment to take off his pants and Keisha removed her's also. He turned off the tv, putting them in complete darkness and slid inside of her—*raw*.

"Yeah baby, you feel that? Damn your pussy good," Rob said as he fucked her. Keisha laid there in silence, she didn't feel a thing; it felt better when they had their clothes on. Out of curiosity she reached her hand down between her legs to see if he was really inside her.

"Uh huh baby, what you doing? I'm about to cum," he said as his breathing got heavy.

"Wait a minute, you don't have a condom on, un huh, get off of me!" she yelled pushing him off of her just as his body started to jerk and his thick cream erupted all over his pubic hair.

"Damn." he took a deep breath and his little dick slowly started to go limp.

'*Damn was right,*' Keisha thought. Disappointed and dissatisfied, what was she gonna do? She couldn't take the pussy back, so she decided to make the best of it and at least try and get some rest next to a warm body for the rest of the night. She snuggled up close to Rob and closed her eyes. Minutes later he nudged her shoulder.

"Come on, you ready? Let me take you home."

Triple Crown Publications presents

CHAPTER 33

Shana was experiencing a burning and itchy sensation in her pussy. More so burning then itching and it was the worse kind of discomfort that she had ever felt in her life. *'I swear if K.C. gave me something, I'll kill his ass,'* she thought. Even though she started making him wear condoms every since he admitted to sleeping around on her, all type of disgusting thoughts crossed her mind. *'What if he gave me something I can't get rid of like herpes or maybe even AIDS.'* Shana loved K.C. and through all his wrong-doing she was still trying to hold on, but if he gave her some kind of sexually transmitted disease she would never be able to forgive him. Sure he fucked around, but she dealt with it as long as he respected her enough to at least use protection. She kept her discomfort from K.C. and held out from sex for a couple of days hoping it would go away, but it didn't. She didn't know which was worse, fighting off K.C. or trying to soothe the irritation with every coohcie cream Duane Reade, CVS and Rite Aid carried. Finally she couldn't take it anymore, so she went to the clinic to find out what was wrong. Going to the department of health was embarrassing, especially since it was located on the Jamaica Ave and everybody hung out on the Ave so the chances of not being seen was slim. Shana paced back in forth in front of the building for about ten minutes before she went inside, but that was the easy part. The hard part was not running into a familiar face while inside the waiting room, because more than likely if you were there it was to treat an STD of some kind.

She quickly scanned the room as she walked over to the front desk to get a number and fill out a questionnaire. She was relieved when she didn't recognize any of the faces. The wait was about an hour before her number was called. Inside the office, the doctor handed her a few STD brochures and asked her all types of questions regarding her sexual history before asking her the nature of her visit. After explaining her discomfort, Shana was asked if she'd like to be tested for HIV.

"No, I just want to know what's causing my irritation," she quickly responded. Shana would not want to live if she found out she had AIDS, so she declined being tested for the virus. The doctor didn't agree with her decision, but didn't push the issue. She told Shana to get undress and lie back on the table. Shana was so uncomfortable. She was 23, married and this was her first GYN check up, ever. The doctor told her to relax and talked her through the examination. In minutes it was over and Shana was told to get dress and return to the waiting room until the nurse called her for blood and urine samples. As she walked down the hallway, reading the information the doctor gave her, someone called out her name.

"Shana!"

Shana's heart dropped when she heard the familiar voice, she looked up and recognized Chasity dressed in one of those two-piece blue hospital uniform as if she worked there. *'Fuck,'* she thought. Out of all people and all the places in the world, why did she have to run into her in here.

"Girl, what are you doing in here?" Chasity said as if everything was cool between them. Shana rolled her eyes and refused to speak at first. Even if they were cool, she thought *'that's the last question I want to be asked right now.'*

"Listen Shana, I know you're probably still mad at me and I don't blame you if you are, but I just want to say I'm sorry for the way I acted. I was just a little hurt you know. Besides, I put dancing and all that other bullshit behind me every since Scar was killed."

"Scar is dead? What happened?" Shana asked.

"I don't really know what happened; I wasn't at the club that night. Supposedly, she left with some guy. who for whatever reason nobody was able to identify and was later found butt-ass naked in a dumpster not far from the club with a slit throat," said Chasity, getting teary eyed.

"This happened at Honey's?"

"Yeah, about a month ago."

"Wow, I'm surprised I didn't hear about that" Shana said.

"I'm not, don't nobody care, to them she's just another trick, but to me she was a good friend, you know. I actually have custody of her daughter, Starlavee, now. She's six."

"Oh okay, I'm sure you'll take good care of her." Shana said.

"Yeah, me and my boyfriend are raising her together."

"Boyfriend." Shana was surprised, she couldn't believe her ears.

"Yes, I have a man now. He's much easier to handle than, you know?" She laughed. Before Shana could respond her number was called again.

"Oh hey, that's me. I gotta go, but you take care. And Chasity, thanks for apologizing." Shana walked into the nurse's office feeling like fifty pounds had just been lifted off her chest.

The nurse took her blood first, then handed her a cup and asked her to go to the bathroom and bring back some urine. Once she brought the urine sample back the nurse gave her a pregnancy test and in minutes a negative result came back. Unfortunately, her discharge sample came back positive for Chlamydia. The nurse told her that it *was* a sexually transmitted disease, but the good new was it was curable. She gave Shana an antibiotic injection and informed her that it would take up to five days for her blood work to come back from the lab confirming whether or not she had any other STDs.

It took a lot to break through Shana's thick skin, but she had just reached her limit with the bullshit. With tears streaming down her face, she wasn't gonna take it no more. She lost herself a long time ago, fucking with K.C., but loving him was no longer worth her dignity. She put up with his ass whippings, his verbal abuse and even his cheating. K.C. owed her more than this, because she was always there for him. Being that down ass bitch wasn't cute no more.

CHAPTER 34

Epiphany was enjoying her time with Wild so much that she didn't want it to end. In twenty-four hours they had already managed to do some much; he bought her a Burberry bikini to swim in amongst other things they picked up during their shopping trip. They also played video games and spent half the night up talking. Her stay felt more like a mini-vacation away from the hood and it made her realize just how much she was ready for some changes in her life. Being with Wild was a different experience for her. He wasn't the cutest nigga, but he had the means to exposed her to a whole new world. Not to mention the other qualities she required, *money, monies* and *more money*!

Wild grew up on the rough streets of Newark, NJ, doing the norm—stealing cars, robbing niggas and hustling—and even thought he was fortunate to make it out the hood, Epiphany admired the fact that he was still street, unlike some niggas, who were quick to switch to that *Hollywood* shit. He also had other characteristics that she admired, like his confidence, sense of humor, and of course his big feet and hands (assuming the myth is true). Wild was feeling Epiphany's personality, which she worked to the fullest. He felt comfortable around her, she didn't appear to be fake like most of the bitches he came across during his success. Plus, she could relate to his struggles and to top it off he found her absolutely gorgeous. Sitting out on the patio smoking weed, Wild entertained Epiphany with crazy stories about the music industry. Quite often, he found himself staring at Epiphany, to him her beauty was such a natural one that made a nigga weak at the knees.

"Epiphany, can you sing?" He asked, thinking if so she'd defiantly give Beyoncé a run for her money.

Epiphany couldn't help but blush, "Sing? No!"

"Come with me." Wild took her by the hand and leading her to his studio.

"I can't sing." Epiphany repeated.

"So, half of the singers out now can't sing. Just go in the booth and sing something into the mic when I tell you to, a'ight?" Epiphany never had a problem with shyness, but she didn't want to embarrass herself.

"Come on girl. Fuck around, you could be the next *J.Lo*," he said cracking a smile.

"Okay here goes nothing." She entered the booth with her all-time favorite song in mind—*'Be happy'* by Mary J.

Wild fumbled with a few buttons on the mixing board before he gave her the okay to sing. Epiphany closed her eyes , tried to catch the tune in her mind and opened her mouth. *'How can I love somebody else, if I can't love myself enough to know when it's time-time to let goooooooooo, sing, all I really want is to be happy to find a love that's mine it would be so sweet.'* Okay that's all I'm giving you of my Mary rendition," she laughed.

"Alright then, that's cool let me see what I could do with that" said Wild. He tried, but was unsuccessful in improving Epiphany's vocals using every voice enhancement key on his computer. "Ahhh, don't go quitting your day job. A'ight?" They both laughed.

Epiphany was having a lot of fun with him, but all this fun was making her horny. She wanted him bad and felt as though she would die from lack of dick if he didn't make a move soon.

She wasn't use to being around a guy for more than ten minutes that didn't try to fuck her. Wild was in the entertainment business, Epiphany had already assumed that he wouldn't be press for pussy since all types of chicks probably came at him. One thing was certain, from his hard-on in the bed last night he was defiantly attracted to her. Still and all, Epiphany wanted to maintain a respectable *'take home to momma'* type of imagine so she fell back on initiating sex of any kind.

Wild sat in his plush leather chair staring at Epiphany, then out of no where he pulled her closer to him and started to fondle her body as though he had read her mind. Epiphany straddled her legs across his lap and stuck her tongue in his mouth, for their first real kiss. *'Damn he can kiss'* she thought as his tongue motion flowed with hers perfectly. Wild started to undress her right there in the studio. He went to unbutton her shirt, but noticed some resistance every time he made an attempt to remove it. She didn't wanted him to go there, but didn't say anything, instead she just redirected his focus by getting down on her knees and releasing his manhood. *'Thank god the myth does apply.'* She opened her mouth and took in as much of his thickness as she possibly could. He was so big that she could only fit half of his dick in her mouth. Just like any pro, Epiphany was up for the challenge. She was determined to taste every inch of him, licking down the sides of his stiffness as he moaned and she lubricated his dick with her saliva, stroking her small hands up and down the base. Wild couldn't take it any longer he wanted to feel inside her walls.

"Ahhh man wait! I want some pussy 'cause I know it's good." Lifting himself up just enough to pull a condom from his back pocket, he passed it to her and smiled. Epiphany stood up and unfastened her Seven jeans. Stepping out of them she slowly rolled the magnum down on his horse sized dick and was ready to ride. "Wait let me see you play with yourself." Wild prolonged insertion as his way of teasing her. Epiphany smiled, she knew the game and played it well as she leaned back on the mixing board and started to lick on her fingers until they shined from her saliva. Then cocking her legs up she slid two of her fingers inside of her and began to moved them in and out of her pussy.

"Ummmmmm" she moaned as her pussy became drenched with juice. Withdrawing her fingers from inside of her, she inserted them in his mouth. Wild sucked on them like they were popsicles and then dove in head first between her legs for more.

"Ooooh, I wanna cum." Epiphany breathed heavily.

"Don't cum yet, I want you to sit on my dick and cum okay."

Without holding back, Epiphany mounted his manhood and slowly stroked him, not quite ready to endure the pain it would've cause if she slammed down on it right away. Not until her pussy's walls adjusted to his fullness, it was on and popping. She worked it, popping her pussy, bouncing up and down on his dick like a wild woman until they both exploded.

CHAPTER 35

Tucker was having a hard time getting use to being without Keisha but he knew moving on was the right thing for him to do. Besides, Leanne was a nice girl with a good head on her shoulders and that somewhat remind him of Keisha. He met her two years ago when she came down to North Carolina with her cousin Josae, one of Mali's jumpoffs. The two hit it off and maintained a platonic relationship for a while until one day Leanne invited him over her to house because she needed to talk, but when he got there she tried to seduce him. Tucker found the whole situation flattering, but at that time his heart belonged to Keisha, and only Keisha, which he explained from the beginning. Embarrassed and rejected, Leanne felt it was best if they ended the friendship and he agreed. News of Malikai's death brought her back into his life. Everything was falling a part for Tucker. Leanne saw an opportunity and went for it, she became the shoulder he needed to lean on, gave him moral support and made him a priority in her life.

Her support kept Tucker sane and for that he was grateful. So, when she arrived at his front door with her bags, he welcomed her with open arms, although he still felt he needed time to get over Keisha. Leanne moved in and wasted no time de-Keishanizing the place and getting rid of everything that had Keisha's name or face on it. The bedroom was repainted, the bathroom and kitchen redecorated and every picture of Keisha was boxed up. Tucker wasn't really happy with the sudden changes she made or her taste but he understood her reasons. She wanted to help him take his mind off the past by all means. Only there was one thing she couldn't erase–his son. Tucker missed his little man so much and without him around everyday was very hard for him. His biggest fear was not being able to be a part of his son's life and to keep that from happening Tucker knew he had to make peace with Keisha. Little man's first birthday was a week away and Tucker wanted him home for the celebration. He picked up the phone and dialed Keisha's cell phone.

"Hello." she answered on the second ring.

"Hey Keish, how's everything?" he asked.

"How do you think?" she answer snidely.

"Look Keish, I ain't call to fight with you okay, I just wanted to know how you was doing and when was our son coming home?"

"I don't know when I'm bringing my son home, I'm homeless remember?"

"Yeah, well you know his birthdays next week?"

"I know, I'm the one that had him."

"Keisha, cut out all the sarcasm, a'ight, are you gonna bring him home or not?"

"That's all you care about, huh?"

"Keisha, he's my son."

"Well, you know what Tucker, when you gave up on me, you gave up him. So, if your not calling me to come back home, he's not coming home either."

"Yo, Keish, what's wrong with you? It's been over a month since he's been gone, he probably don't even remember us. You think you're getting back at me with your bullshit, but you're punishing him too. I never thought you could be such a fucked up person Keisha, but I swear to you, if you think your gonna use my son against me or even try to keep him from me, I will fucking kill you. Do you hear me?"

"Is that a threat Tucker, you're gonna fucking kill me, huh? Well come on muthafucka kill me, 'cause you ain't never gon' see your son again. We're a package deal sweetie, so if I ain't got you, then you ain't got a son. You got that! Besides, I heard you got a new girl. Tell her to give you a fucking son and leave mines alone!" Keisha screamed right before she slammed down the phone. Tucker was hot with Keisha, he tried calling her back but she wouldn't answer her phone. He buried his head in his hands thinking how Keisha must have really lost her mind if she thinks he's gonna go for her bullshit.

"Baby are you okay?" asked Leanne after overhearing his conversation with Keisha. Tucker let out a hard sigh as he lifted up his head.

"Nah, she's trying to keep me from my son now."

"What! Baby you can't let her do that to you, you're his father and you have just as much rights as she does. What you need to do is just go get him." Leanne suggested.

"I just don't know why she had to go and fuck up everything," said Tucker.

"Well baby, everything happens for a reason and at least you found out her true colors before you two got married. Now are you gonna sit here and regret what you can't change or are we gonna go get your son." She ran her fingers through Tuckers hair and secretly hated the fact that he still had feelings for Keisha.

"What would I do with out you?" Tucker stood up and gave her a tight hug. "Come on, let's go get my little man."

CHAPTER 36

Epiphany woke up and instantly went into a funk after over hearing Wild booking a flight for leaving for LA that night. Her little vacation with him was over before she was ready for it to be. She wondered if he would ever call her again and hoped that her time spent with him wasn't a complete waste because yes she had a great time, but she wasn't doing it for nothing. Epiphany wanted to be rescued from the hood by a wealthy knight in platinum armor and live glamorously and happily ever after. That was the ghetto fairytale she was hoping for.

"Good morning, Beautiful." Wild said as he plopped down next to her on the bed. Right off the back he sensed a bit of attitude by the way she twisted up her lips and cut her eyes at him. "What up, you okay?" he asked.

"Yeah, I'm okay." She lied.

"You don't seem okay, so tell me what's wrong."

"Nothing, I just overheard you making travel plans, and I guess I wasn't ready for it to be over with us." Epiphany said.

"Oh, so it's over between us?" Wild questioned.

"I don't know, you tell me." She answered.

"Nah, as long as you don't want it to be over it ain't."

155

"And what do you want?" Epiphany asked.

"Well first, I wanna know why you won't let me kiss on your tits?"

"Wild, come on be serious!"

"I *am* serious, I wanna know why every time we had sex you did everything to deter me from seeing them." He thought that maybe she had gotten a bad boob job or something of that nature.

Epiphany's eyes started to tear up, he was right, she did stop him from removing her shirt every time they had sex, but it wasn't because of her tatas it was because of the ugly scar she was hiding. She really didn't know how she was gonna to explain it, slowly removing her shirt, she thought of an explanation.

"What happen to you?" he questioned in shock. Epiphany revealed the ugly scar from not only the bullet but the surgery she had done on her lung.

"I was in an abusive relationship and when I tried to leave him, he tried to kill me." Epiphany said.

"Damn ma, I'm sorry to hear that, where's his punk ass at now?"

"I don't know." Epiphany answered.

"What you mean, you don't know? Come on, for some sucker shit like that he should be under the fucking jail."

"I know, but it didn't turn out that way. Believe me, I wish it did because maybe then the nightmares would stop and I wouldn't have to worry about him coming back for me one day. But you know, with you I feel safe, I haven't even thought about it." Her tears continued to fall. Epiphany over-dramatized her story to gain his sympathy and it worked. Wild seen a lot of crazy shit go down in his hood when it came to a man and his girl, so Epiphany's story wasn't far fetched. He could understand a nigga not wanting to let her go because she was absolutely gorgeous, but what she did for him was more mental then physical. He fucked plenty of pretty girls with good pussy, but with Epiphany he felt a connection that was real and that made him want to hold on to her.

"Listen Epiphany, I'm feeling you like crazy and if you feel like I feel and it ain't about the money, then maybe something serious could pop off. I'll be in LA for a couple of weeks, but when I get back, I'm trying to see what's good, a'ight?" He leaned down and kissed her ugly scar. Epiphany didn't say a word she just looked in his eyes and hoped her tearful emotions would say it all, but in her mind she was screaming *'I got his ass.'* Just like that old school tune said, *'Use what you got to get what you want.'* All she could think about was a life filled with the finer things like shopping sprees, VIP status, trips around the world and maybe even a career in acting.

Triple Crown Publications presents

CHAPTER 37

C-God lost himself completely as his addiction started to control his mind, body and soul. His body started to take on the form of a true fiend as well as his habits. His money was spent, his jewelry sold and the only other thing he possessed that held any value, his Cadillac Escalade, was dogged out by the local street corner dealers, who he let drive it more than him in exchange for crack. Marisa lost her kids to the system due to her neglect and started selling pussy to any nigga that would provide her and C with their next hit. C-God started asking Reggie to wire him money on the regular until Reggie just started ignoring his calls. Tanya had no idea that he was cracked out, so she would send him a couple of dollars whenever she could, until she started to suspect something was up. It got to the point where he would call at all times of the day wanting her to go to a Money Gram. He'd make up all kinds of excuses for why he couldn't see her. Eventually, she washed her hand of him. C-God was smoked out and all he had was his memories of when he was getting paper. He would tell his story to any young hustler, in VA, who was willing to listen to him talk about what he used to have, how one of his own betrayed him, shaming him and his family's name. Nigga's didn't believe or respect him at first, they would clown him and his stories.

"Ahh go head with that shit, nigga you ain't nothing but a crackhead." They would say. It wasn't until he started to drop some valuable knowledge, rules to the game that could be beneficial to one's progression, that they really paid attention and respected the shit he was saying. One particular nigga named Alpo, a lightweight in the game, had enough hunger to be a heavyweight and took a liking to C-God. He could tell C knew exactly what he was talking about, concerning this drug shit. Even though he was a fallen soldier, Alpo still admired the position he once held. During a two year bid in prison, he became real familiar with the reputation of the infamous Hinderson brothers from some stories cats told. C-God also took a liking to Alpo because he reminded him of himself eight years ago at the ripe age of twenty-two. He seen a similar hunger in him and felt, given the right type of guidance, Alpo would not only be official, but he could be what C-God tried to be—unstoppable.

CHAPTER 38

On the way home Shana rehearsed her "I'm leaving you" speech over and over again. It was gonna be hard to face K.C. without trying to claw his fucking eyes out, but at this point it was whatever she thought. Her cell phone started ringing, but no number registered on the screen. She debated for a moment on whether or not she should answer it.

"Hello?" she finally answered.

"Yo Cream, they got me locked up," said Raina.

"What?" Shana had been caught off guard.

"Yo, it's me Raina, they raided Honey's last night. I had your shit on me and got locked the fuck up. I'm at the Queens House so ante up and get me out of here, my bail is five thousand."

"A'ight, I got you." Shana said nonchalantly. *'Damn, what next?'*

"I hope so, because if you have me in here too long, I'ma start talking." Raina hung up before Shana could respond.

When Shana walked in the apartment K.C. was on the phone but her anger towards him was now diverted towards getting that bitch Raina out of jail. She cut her eyes at him as hard as she could to let him know they had beef, while passing him to get to the bedroom.

"Yo Smitty, my chick stay mad at me dawg," K.C. said noticing her attitude. Shana slammed the bedroom door, she despised Smitty's ass, too. Plopping down on the foot of the bed she tossed her car keys to the side and just sat for a moment, thinking about Raina's threat to snitch her out. The more she contemplated the more she realized that Raina ain't have nothing on her but her stage name. She didn't know her real name and if she did she didn't know her full name, or where she lived or anything about her connect. She was no longer worried.

'If I was a complete bitch I'd let her ass hang' Shana thought getting up and walking over to the closet for her stash. She could still hear K.C. on the phone with Smitty, but didn't pay their conversation any mind until she heard Epiphany's name being mentioned. Pressing her ear up against the door she eavesdropped on what K.C. was saying.

"Who, Epiphany? Nah, I don't think she got it back, if so don't you think she would of had the police all over Ness's ass for that shit. What? I think so. Come on man; the nigga tried to kill her. Yo, that's your boy. Nah I can't even fuck with him like that no more. Yeah, he be bugging the fuck out and I know that nigga is responsible for what happened to Righteous and his girl. Yo, you still asking about that bitch? Yo, man let it go. Nah Shana ain't gon' hook that shit up. She can't stand ya ass, besides Shana don't even fuck with her like that no more and what's up with you and my sister? Yeah you right, Trina is a crazy bitch. But yo, what's up with that money? Nah, I got mine ready nigga. I'm waiting on yours."

From the sound of it, Shana assumed Ness was the one responsible for Epiphany's brush with death. *'That dude Ness rubbed me the wrong way just by looking at him. Damn he probably did Mali too and what the fuck is up with Smitty wanting to get with Epiphany? That ain't happening, he's not even in her league. when I met him the first time, he claimed he already fucked her and couldn't stand her, so what's really good? Today is defiantly just one of those days.'* Shana directed her attention back to her stash in the closest. Pulling down the timberland shoe box she notice it felt extremely light. Shana opened the box and instantly she noticed the dent in her savings. What use to be 42g's was now only two-thousand dollars. Shana threw the shoe box on the floor, dug in the back of the closet and pulled out one of those metal baseball bats and stormed out into the living room.

"Where that fuck is my money at, huh?" she screamed.

"Whoa, whoa, yo nigga I'm a hit you back." K.C. quickly hung up the phone "Yo Sha, chill the fuck out!" He yelled making a move to grab the bat. Shana stepped back and swung with all her strength, '*whack*,' hitting his arm.

"Don't fuck with me K.C. Where the fuck is my money you dirty dick nigga?"

"OUCH! Yo what the hell is wrong with you, Sha? Shana positioned herself to slug his ass again. "Yo, chill, don't hit me no more!" He ordered as if he was in any position to make demands.

"K.C. I swear on everything I love, if you don't give me my money right now I'm gonna take this fucking bat and try to kill you with it."

"Sha, listen I just need a couple of weeks. Let me make this move with Smitty and, I promise you, I'll give you back double. Come on Ma, put the bat down. Just grind with me please, so I can get this paper, a'ight? Come on Sha, you know I got you. Clyde can't shine without Bonnie."

Shana did the math, double meant eighty grand. She weighed out her options,

'*Raina's bail or a forty-thousand dollar profit*' *Fuck Raina* she thought lowering the bat.

"See, that's why I love you girl." K.C. let out a hard sigh of relief. Shana turned up her lips and gave him a '*Whatever nigga*' look.

"Well if you love me like that then go get your dirty dick cured and stop fucking them nasty ass hoes." She walked back in the bedroom, slamming and locking the door behind her. Shana laid on the bed trying hard to understand how and why she loved K.C. grimey ass so much.

CHAPTER 39

Epiphany's mother was glad that she was home and still in one piece considering that she hadn't heard from her in days. Really, she wanted to talk to Epiphany about Keisha's recent behavior, thinking maybe she could talk some sense into her friend. Lord knows she tried, Keisha was like a daughter to her and she couldn't sit back and watch her live recklessly.

"Epee, I need to talk to you," Mrs. Wright was obviously worried.

"Ma, before you start, I'm sorry I didn't call, but I was fine." Epiphany answered defensively.

"I can see that now, but you know what, I'm not gonna go there with you. I wanna talk about Keisha."

"What about Keisha, is she here?"

"Shhh, she's downstairs."

"Okay well, what happened?"

"Epee, I'm worried about her, she been running out of here with a different guy every night for the past four days, and you know that ain't like her."

"Ma, she's just trying to get her mind off of Tucker that's all.

It's not that big of a deal." Epiphany tried to justify Keisha's behavior.

"Well, I tried talking to her and I'm telling you, she's not herself. She hasn't even mentioned her son."

"Ma, I'm sure she's fine, but if you want I'll talk to her. Don't worry about lil' Tucker's. He's with her mom in Atlanta. I'm going downstairs now." Epiphany whined.

"I'll tell you this, you girls need to except Christ in you life and stop running around here taking things for granted. Your father's trying to."

"Yeah, yeah, yeah. Where's daddy at anyway?" Epiphany asked heading down the basement steps.

"He went to see his brother. Your Uncle Ramel got arrested? Um hum, the Feds finally caught up with him."

"Wow that's too bad." Epiphany said sarcastically.

"What's up E? It's about time you came home girl" Keisha excitedly sat up on her futon bed anticipating the 411 on Epiphany's new friend.

"Hey, I know. Believe me it wasn't by choice and it ain't for long. Wild's gonna take me up out of the hood." Epiphany said with a smiled.

"Are you serious? So what happened? He must have a lot of money 'cause I ain't seen you smile like that since your father bought you that beamer."

"Keish, he has everything I want in a man; a lot of money, a huge house, good dick, no kids and he's not cheap at all. He bought me this Marc Jacobs bag for $725. This fucking bag is a month's rent and I'm walking around with it on my arm. I ain't never had a purse that cost more then five hundred dollars. So girl, you know I made it my business to put it on his ass, right? 'Cause shit, a bitch is trying to get a one way ticket out of Southside, okaaay!"

"That's good, I'm so happy for you." Keisha was a little envious. She once had everything she wanted in a man, too, and she missed the feeling.

"Anyway enough about me, how was your date with that guy?" Epiphany asked.

"Which one?" Keisha answered.

"Well damn Keish, go on brush your shoulders off. I'm scared of you," laughed Epiphany.

"Don't be, because my pimp game sucks." Keisha sighed.

"Well, what happen to the computer fix-it-guy?"

"Oh my gosh, E, his apartment was a dump, his ding–a-ling was the size of my son's and now he has the audacity to avoid my calls."

"The dick was trash and your still calling him, why?"

"I don't know."

"Well, did he at least take you out and spend some money?"

"Out? Out for him was a movie in his junkie ass one-room apartment."

"Keish I know you been out of the loop for a minute, but did you not learn anything from me? If your gonna give it up get something out of it, okay!"

"I know, I had sex with three guys in the last four days and none of them made me cum. It's like I'm going from bad to worst." Keisha confessed.

"*Three guys*, from where Keisha?"

"Blackplanet.com."

"Are you crazy, Keisha!"

"No, I'm just lonely."

"So, why don't you call to see how T's doing?"

"For what? He hates me."

"Keish, I'm talking about your son. When was the last time you called to check on him and when is he coming home?" Not waiting for Keisha's response Epiphany handed her the phone.

"I don't know E, maybe in a couple of days or so, I just haven't been feeling like a mom ever since Tucker left me. It's almost like I had a baby for him and now that he's gone I don't want my son anymore. I guess I should at least call." Keisha hesitantly dialing her mom's number. Epiphany knew Keisha was hurting inside, but she couldn't believe what was coming out of her mouth and chose not to comment.

"Hello?" answered one of Keisha's sisters.

"Hi, this is Keisha whose this?"

"Hey gurl, this Kelly."

"What up Kells, how's my son doing?"

"He ain't here."

"What, then where is he?"

"I don't know. Didn't you send Tucker here to get him?"

"No, I didn't. Where is Loretta at?"

"She ain't here. Tucker took the baby two days ago, he said you told him to come pick him up," said Kelly.

"Well I didn't, I have to go–bye!" Keisha hung up and immediately started dialing Tucker's cellphone, then the house phone, but got no answer.

"What happened Keish, is lil' T okay?" Epiphany asked.

"I don't know, he's not there, he's with Tucker." she answered.

"Tucker went to ATL and got him and you didn't know anything about it?"

"No I didn't and I can't understand why Loretta would let Tucker just take him like that without consulting with me first. Now Tucker's not answering his phone." Keisha took a moment to think. "Epiphany, do you think he's trying to take my son from me?"

"I don't know, but maybe you need to just go over there and see what's up. You could take my car unless you want me to go with you."

"No you don't have to, but thanks." Keisha said as she took Epiphany car keys.

When she arrived to what use to be her home, Tucker' s car along with a light blue Honda Accord was parked in the driveway. Keisha got out the car and walked up the steps, she could see the that lights were on through the front window and proceeded to repeatedly press the bell, causing it to sing an annoying *'ding dong, ding dong'* tune. Her heart pounded as she impatiently waited all of two minutes. *'If I have to start breaking windows around this muthafucka, I'll do it. My presence is gonna be felt,'* she thought. She prepared herself to take it there if she had to. Just as Keisha step down off the steps in search of a nice size rock with some weight to it, Tucker answer the door in a sweat, looking like he was getting his work out on. He was wearing a pair of Calvin Klein drawstring pajama pants, with no shirt and scratches on his chest.

"What do you want?" An annoyed Tucker watched her search the grass. Keisha looked up and saw him at the door.

"I came to get my son!"

"Keisha, I'm a take care of him from now on. You shipped him off and forgot about him, remember that? It took you two fucking days to find out I had him? Just continue to do you. My little man is straight, right here with me."

"I don't care if took me five days, I came to get my son and I'm not leaving without him."

"Keisha, just go a'ight!"

"No, I'm not gonna *just go*. What the fuck were you doing anyway and whose car is that? I know your not stupid enough to have some bitch around my son."

"Whatever Keish, goodbye." Tucker went back inside the house and slammed the door.

"Tucker, you better give me my fucking son, or I swear you'll be sorry!" Keisha screamed, but Tucker didn't come back to the door. "Oh so you want me to take it there, huh?" Keisha walked across the front lawn, once again for a rock. She couldn't find a rock but spotted some bricks that were stacked next to the fence in the front lawn. Loosening three bricks from the soil she slammed one into the windshield of the Honda, then the passengers side window of Tucker's 745 and the third brick she threw crashed right through the center of the house's front window, setting off both car alarms and the ADT system. Keisha was turning into some crazed madwomen, screaming vulgar obscenities and threw a raging tantrum in the front of the house. She wanted her son, but what really set her off was the assumption that Tucker had a girl inside the house with him. Tucker was furious, his tolerance had just exceed its limited. Baby momma or no baby momma he was gonna beat that ass.

Running out of the house, Tucker charge right at Keisha and tackled her. Releasing all the anger and pain he was holding in, he literally tried to strangle the life out of Keisha. The upper class neighborhood they lived in wasn't use to such disturbances, so instantly many of their neighbors peaked from their window to see what the commotion was about, some even called police. But not one of them came over and tried to get Tucker off of her. Leanne ran out the house and tried to pull him off of Keisha, but he was so worked up that he shoved her so hard she went flying across the grass. It was the sound of his son's cry that caused him to free Keisha from his choke hold. Breathing heavily, Tucker got off of her and rushed over to the door to calm and console his son. Keisha eyes were bloodshot and watery as she coughed and wheezed, trying to catch her breath. Once she gained control of her breathing, she heard a recognizable female's voice.

"Baby are you okay?" Lea's face fit the voice and seeing her set Keisha off again. She jumped up from the ground and attacked her from behind. Grabbing Lea by her long frizzy half-black, half-white mixed hair, she tossed her to the ground and ferociously punched her face. It happen so fast that Tucker couldn't come to her rescue right away, he was holding his son. Running in the house, Tucker secured lil' T safely in his stroller and came back out to her rescue, but by the time he made it back out front the police had arrived and already controlled the situation. After questioning the three of them, all fingers pointed to Keisha as the villain. Tucker decided not to press charges but Lea did so Keisha was hauled off to jail and charged with aggravated assault, disruptive behavior and disturbing the peace.

CHAPTER 40

Shana stared at the ceiling half of the night, restless, she tossed and turned. Raina's threats, her STD results, K.C.'s infidelity and her money investment with him, was all way too much to grasp. Through it all, one thing troubled her the most—K.C.'s phone conversation earlier. Despite felling that Epiphany was a complete bitch, who worked every nerve in her body,(plus, she had enough problems of her own not to get involved in someone else's) she knew her conscience would only eat away at her if she kept quite about it. Not only did she feel Epiphany had every the right to know what really went down, she also felt, without a doubt, Ness should pay for his actions. Shana glanced at the clock on the nightstand and read 12:45am. She got out the bed, still fully dress from earlier. Without turning on the lights she felt around the bed for her car keys which were still at the foot of the bed were she had left them. She unlocked and slowly opened the bedroom door, peeking out she saw K.C. on the couch asleep with the tv watching him. *'Thank God,'* she thought. The last thing she wanted to hear was his mouth. Shana left the house, went for a drive and ending up in front of Epiphany's house. She called her on her cell.

"Hello?" Epiphany answered half asleep.

"What's up E, I need to holla at you about something." Shana said.

"Whose this?"

"It's Shana, come outside."

"Shana I'm sleeping."

"E, C-God ain't do it."

"What?" Epiphany's voice got louder.

"C-god ain't the one that shot you, but since you sleeping fuck it."

"No wait, I'm coming." Epiphany was awake now. She hung up, hopped out of bed, threw on some sweats, slippers and headed out the side door. Opening Shana's passenger side door, she got in eagerly anticipating what she had to say.

"What's going on, Shana?"

"Listen, I know who shot you. I don't know him like that but he be with K.C. and this guy name Smitty."

"Well, who is he and how is he linked to me?"

"His name is Ness, he use to run with C-God."

"So, how do you know he's the one that shot me?" asked Epiphany.

"Look, that's not important, I just know, okay?"

"What about Malikai, is he the one that killed him too?"

"More than likely, but listen his boy Smitty is feeling you hard so I was thinking maybe you should fuck with the nigga just to manipulate the situation, try to turn him against Ness. That way he could take care of him for you." Shana suggested.

"I don't know, I think I should just put all this behind me. I mean what's done is done. Besides, I'm trying to get up out of here anyway."

"What! Come on, I know you ain't trying to let that nigga get away with this bullshit, Epiphany. The muthafucka left you for dead and you wanna put that behind you?"

"Shana, I almost died and that shit scares me. I ain't trying get caught up in some bullshit with the same muthafucka that tried to kill me. And anyway, what's it to you? You act like your the one with the vendetta."

"What, I'm trying to look out for you, but if you don't feel like your life is worth getting payback, fuck it then! Have a good-night." Shana turned the tables on Epiphany. Of course she had her motives but she couldn't disclose that.

"Yeah, whatever," Epiphany slammed the car door behind her and headed back to the house. Inside, she glanced over at Keisha empty bed and briefly wondered where she could be at that time of night. Sitting up on her bed, she thought about what Shana said and the dream she had at Keisha's house. There were two male voices present the night she was shot. Epiphany sat in the dark, deep in her thoughts, for more than twenty minutes when suddenly, the sounds of Prince's *'Do me baby,'* Mali and her laughing and the moment she froze from shock when she saw the bullet pierce through his skull flashed in her mind. She could remember the splattered blood mixed with pieces of Mali's brain sprinkle all over her and the way her body trembled as she stood still in fear watching his body slump over to the side. C-God ordered the trigger man he called Ness to search her crib. She could feel the enormous amount of pain she experienced that night all over again as her tears began to fall. Epiphany rehashed everything that took place that night, from the verbal to the physical abuse she was subjected to and the reason it all took place. She remembered all the horrific details that lead her to squeeze the trigger of her nine with the intent to kill C-God. It was Ness that entered the room and blasted off his .38 in C's defense, successfully hitting her in the chest and sending her into a state of unconsciousness.

CHAPTER 41

Keisha cried the whole ride over to Central Booking. She couldn't believe Lea actually played her like that. *'How long has she known him?'* Keisha wondered. Putting two and two together she realized how well Lea smoothly played everything off. She made it seem like she only liked Spanish guys and always claimed to have a man. She'd say anything to cover up the fact that she was a jealous, man-stealing, backstabbing bitch. Keisha felt like such an idiot for letting her guard down and befriending Lea. She told her personal things about her and Tucker's sex life; his dick size, how he was always away from home and even about her alter ego, BAPS, that she used in the dirty online chat rooms. She had to admit she set herself up for the kill, played right into Lea's hands. She agreed to her inviting strippers that night, when in her heart she was dead set against whole the idea.

By the time Keisha finished getting processed it was too late to stand before a judge. Although it was late she decided to use her one phone call to call Mrs. Wright, she was certain she'd reach her. She explained her situation to Mrs. Wright and told her that she wouldn't know anything further regarding her release until the morning, which meant she had to spend the night in the bullpen. Keisha had never experienced such filth in her life, locked up with prostitutes, drug addicts, boosters and God only knew what else. It was a tight squeeze in the overcrowded cell. With one dingy stall in the corner, the men in the other cell directly across could see everything. The idea of having to stay in a place like this turned her stomach. There was one long wooden bench up against the wall that was so full, women were stretched out in the remaining three corners and all over the floor. With no place to rest, she though she'd be standing in that one spot for the remainder of the night.

"Here honey, come sit next to big Doris." A woman said, patting a small space next to her on the bench. Detecting Keisha hesitation she continued, "Come honey, I ain't gon' bite you, shit I got daughters your age." That made Keisha feel a little more at ease, hopefully Big Doris wasn't on no lesbo shit. She proceeded towards her.

"Thanks," Keisha said sitting down.

"No problem honey, what you in here for?" Big Doris asked.

"Ahhh …I had a fight with this backstabbing bitch that stole my man." Keisha was still bitter. All of a sudden she noticed all the track marks and sores on every visible part of Big Doris's body.

"Honey you are too nice of a good looking girl to be fighting over some damn man. And I'm a tell you just like I tell my own girls *'if you got to fight over a man then he ain't yours.'* Now look you in here and he's probably with that heifer."

Keisha explained to Big Doris that the situation was much deeper, because they had a child together. Big Doris told her she understood and advised that if a situation calls for her to move on, then that's what she should do. Keisha revealed how Lea had betrayed her and that's when Big Doris changed her tune. *"You should beat that bitch with a bat every time you see the hoe!"* Keisha was enjoying her conversation with Big Doris, she had a great sense of humor, plus she knew a lot of shit about life. Talking to her made the hours go by a little faster despite the fact that she would nod off for at least thirty seconds in between each sentence and pick at the nasty scabs on her arm and neck exposing the tendencies of a true dope fiend.

Finally, morning came and Keisha's name was called to stand before the judge. As soon a she entered the courtroom she spotted Mrs. Wright seated, hopefully waiting to take her home. No doubt she was happy to she her, but she was also expecting Tucker to be present as well. Unfortunately that didn't happen and she couldn't hold back her tears from the pain she was feeling. The judge released her on her own recognizance and scheduled for her to appear back in court in three weeks.

CHAPTER 42

C-god continued to school his new student, Alpo, about the hustling game. Even though C-God was still getting high as kite, the two became kind of close. Alpo looked at him as somewhat of a mentor, while C-God viewed Alpo as his prodigy; he had heart, will and a hunger that could take him far. C-God wanted to help him prosper, but he needed something done for him first. Alpo was down for C-God's revengeful plan. He ran the necessary questions by Alpo—had he ever caught a body before and whether or not he was afraid too. C wanted to personally see to it Ness's suffered, he also needed to know that if Alpo had to pull the trigger he wouldn't bitch up. Alpo assured him that he had his back. All C-God had to do was say when and how he wanted the shit to go down. C-god mapped out the whole thing weeks ago. Next, all he had to do was get a hold of Reggie, who was still ducking C-God calls, even though he left messages that it wasn't about money but rather another very important matter. Reg figured he somehow got word that he and Tanya were in a relationship and he wasn't ready to face C with that yet. Once again he'd betrayed C-God, this time falling in love with one of his baby mothers and he didn't know how he was going to explain that. C-god asked him to look after her and now they were living together. In order for his plan to be carried out C-God was willing to ignore Reggie's shitting on him. He needed him as an inside connect and felt Reggie owned him that much.

CHAPTER 43

Epiphany replayed that deadly night over and over again in her head for the last couple of days. It was clear now, Ness was the one responsible for Malikai's death and her being shot. Focused on noting but her newfound recollection, Wild's phone calls were the only thing that made her feel better. He would phone her whenever he got a break from the music just to let her know she was in his thoughts Their relationship was quickly growing strong and he made it clear that he wanted to take things to the next level by asking her to come live with him. Epiphany wasted no time giving him her answer, she excitingly blurted out *"Yes"* without putting any thought into it. She didn't care whether or not it was too soon or if it would even work out. Love had nothing to do with it. All she wanted was to leave the hood and to live her life in a rich man's world. But first, as much as her gut was telling her to move on and put her past behind her, she just couldn't until Ness paid for what he did to her and Malikai. After putting as much thought into it as she possibly could, she phone Shana.

"What's up." Shana answered recognizing Epiphany's number from the caller id.

"Shana listen, I've been thinking about what you said and your right, that son of a bitch has to pay for trying to take my life away."

"So what, you ready to fuck with Smitty?" Shana questioned.

"Yeah if he's the one that could help me?"

"Hell yeah, he's the one, plus he got it bad for you, E. All you gotta do is get the nigga open and I'm telling you he'll probably do what whatever you want him to."

"But, if Ness is his boy, how am I gonna get him to get at 'em for me?" Epiphany asked.

"Come on E, good pussy can make a nigga do anything. This is me you talking too and I know you know how too put it down for your crown. Just manipulate the shit out of his ass and make him think you feeling him like that, then set him up for the kill."

"A'ight, I got you."

"Cool, I'ma set it up, so expect his call a'ight!"

"Okay!" Ending the call Epiphany felt jitters, she was a little nervous about the plan, *'It has to work,'* she thought, 'because nobody fucks over Epiphany Janee Wright and gets away with it'.

Shana wasted no time getting on it. As soon as she got off the phone with Epiphany, she phoned Smitty and made arrangements to meet with him at IHOP for breakfast. He agreed. Shana got up, showered and dressed. On her way out the door she glance over and rolled her eyes disgusted with K.C. He was on the couch were he's been sleeping for the past couple of nights, since she began her silent treatment. When she got in her car she turned on her cell phone and retrieved the six messages that were waiting for her.

Message one: *"Yeah bitch, I see you trying to front on me huh? A'ight hoe, I'ma see you!"* Message two: *"Yo Cream, I see your sheisty ass really ain't trying to get me outta here, huh? Watch your back bitch!"* Message three: *"Shana Scott how bout this, you can ignore my calls all you want, but my peoples will be seeing you, a'ight!"* Messages four, five and six were pretty much the same. Raina went from calling her Cream to her government name and admitted she knew who her man was and where they lived. Now, Shana was starting to fret. She pulled up to the IHOP, went inside and was seated. Of course, Smitty had her waiting for over thirty minutes and when he arrived he was freshly dipped in a Rocawear sweatsuit, all white uptowns, a pair of at least 4 caret diamond earrings and a platinum link chain with an iced out Jesus head on it (Shana never understood how a nigga out to do so much dirt could walk around sporting Jesus on a chain). *'Look at this character,'* she thought, pissed off assuming that her money probably paid for all his shit.

"Sha-money, what up girl?" Smitty smiled as he slid into the booth next to her.

"What's up, why you always gotta keep a bitch waiting, huh?"

"Yo, what's up? Oh wait, let me order some food first—a nigga starving." Smitty looked at the menu, disregarding her attitude and her question. The two ordered breakfast before Shana began to conduct business.

"Listen, I know you heard that the police ran up in Honey's and shut shit down, right?" Shana asked.

"Nah, when this happened?" Shana knew he was lying, but didn't call him on it, she just continued on about Raina getting caught up in the sweep.

"A'ight, so why is you telling me?" Smitty questioned.

"I'm telling you 'cause the bitch is locked the fuck up and she's making threats to snitch me out. Her bail is 5g's and I ain't got it and if I ain't got that, then you know I ain't got the money to keep paying your fucking ass for that bullshit you got on me. Don't you think we played this game long enough? Me and K.C. ain't working out, but I'm willing to do you a favor if you could front me the money for Raina's bail and after I pay you back we're even." Smitty laughed at her.

"What kind of favor you gon' do for me that's gonna cost me

5g's. That shit sounds funnier than a muthafucka!" He said. "Anyway what's up with your E connect. Honey's ain't the only strip joint you could sell them shits at?"

"I know that, but my connect ain't fucking with me no more. The last time I went to checked him he told me that that was my last play 'cause he was giving it up and moving to Vegas." Shana lied, truth be told *she* didn't want to do it anymore, but she knew if she told Smitty that, his greed would get in the way. She no longer cared about him telling K.C. about Chasity, besides Chasity had a man now. But, she knew that Smitty would dig up some more dirt to hold against her because he's that kind of nigga. She wanted all debts settled.

"Oh word, so if that stripper bitch ain't get knocked you still would of been ass out huh?" Smitty asked.

"Yeah I guess, but at least I would of had the doe she made for the week. Anyway, that's neither here nor there—do we got a deal or not?" Shana questioned.

"Yo, I ain't hear no deal? What I'm giving you 5g's for and why you ain't ask my man K.C.?"

"Cause he's the reason I ain't got it! Remember, ya'll little investment? Don't worry, as soon as I get my cut from him, I give you my word, I'll give it back to you. You feeling my homegirl, Epiphany, right? I could hook that up for you, you know wash my back and I'll wash yours!"

"Get the fuck out of here," he laughed. "You want me to pay you for that. Yo, she already tried that. And I'ma tell you like I told her, 'The kid don't pay for no pussy' A'ight, yo!"

"I'm not asking you to pay for nothing, are you listening? I said loan! C'mon Smitty, one good deed deserves another. You been hitting my pockets hard. There's gotta be a reason why you wanted me to hook you and Epiphany up, so what is it? You already hit it, so why don't you just step to her again?"

"Yo, shit went sour between us—that's all."

"So, she don't remember shit about you." Shana said.

"For real, that shit's really true about her losing her memory?"

"Yeah."

"No bullshitting?"

"Nah, no bullshit, so that means whatever happened between ya'll don't even matter. You got a clean slate homie." Shana assured him.

"So shit, I could holla at her myself then." Smitty respond.

"Yeah you could, but she kind of leery about fucking with around the way niggas now. I'll let her know shit is cool and you'se my nigga, so she might rock with you."

"It's like that, with just your word. K.C. told me ya'll ain't rock like that no more."

"He don't know what the fuck he be talking about. First off, the nigga stay too busy fucking other bitches to know who I'm cool with. Epiphany is my girl, we been cool for over ten years. You trying to holla at her or what?"

"Well, I don't know what you talking about as far as my man with other girls, but yeah I'm trying to swing with that." Smitty tried his best to cover up for K.C.

"A'ight cool," Shana ignored his bold face lie. "So, when you gon' give me the money?" She continued.

"When you hook that up!"

"Come on Smitty, don't fucking try to play me."

"Yo, I'm not. I'm trying to get at her." Smitty said.

"Then when you give me the money, I'll call her, so you could do that."

"What you don't trust me?" Shana didn't answer, she just gave him a look. *'Nigga that's an understatement.'*

"A'ight, a'ight." He got the message. I'll have it for you later on today. When I call you be ready to meet up, a'ight? Smitty got up from the table and left, leaving her stuck with the bill. Shana just shook her head. *'What a desperate thirsty muthafucka!'*

CHAPTER 44

It took everything Mrs. Wright had in her to convince Keisha not to go back over to Tucker's house and confront Lea. She told Keisha that she needed to cool out for a couple of days, then take the police over there to get her son. Keisha agreed, but the thought of her son being around another women ate away at her. Blocking her number she called the house. The phone rang three times before Lea answered.

"Hello."

Keisha fumed with anger when she heard that bitch answer the phone, but she tried hard to keep her composure because she didn't want to get hung up on.

"Can I please speak to Tucker? She asked grinding her teeth and breathing heavy. Lea wasn't going to hang up because she wanted the opportunity to rub her shit in Keisha's face.

"Do you mean my Tucker or your little rugrat?"

"What did you just say, bitch!" Keisha yelled.

"You heard what I said Keisha. Are you calling for my man or that fucking little brat of yours." Lea taunted.

"I know, Tucker must not be there because if he heard you talking about our son like that— that's right I repeat *our son*— your ass would be out of there so fast, bitch."

189

"Oh, you think so? You know what, Keisha, your such a stupid ass little hoe. You fell right into my trap, dummy. I set the whole thing up. You ever wonder why you got tipsy so fast, hum? I spiked your drink with Ez-lay and you got laid. The Damager's a male prostitute, a gigolo. It only cost me $300 to destroy your perfect little relationship."

"You fucking bitch! Why would you do that to me? What did I ever do to you besides trust you as my friend." Keisha couldn't control the sadness in her voice.

"Honestly, Keisha, it had nothing to do with you. I met Tucker way before I even knew who you were. I liked him, but he told me that he had a girl that he loved so he couldn't get down like that. At first I was pissed off, I felt rejected and I let it go. Then fate would have it, I ended up going to the same college and becoming friends with you. Funny thing is, I didn't even realize who you were when you started yapping your gums about how good Tucker was and the lavish wedding you were planning. That is, until you showed me his picture. I wanted to tell you I knew him, but then you started complaining about all the problems you were having with him. That was the break I needed. And you know what Keisha, you were right, the sex is *incredible*. Keisha was appalled, enraged and speechless. She sat lifeless listening to Lea humiliate her. Tucker walked in and Lea switched it up, quick fast. "Oh honey your just in time. Keisha's on the phone. Here, let me take lil' man, so you two can talk, okay baby? No honey, talk to her for lil' man's sake, you have too." Tucker must have refused to talk to her cause all she heard next was the dial tone. From that point on, Keisha realized she was up against a real live one and she needed to get her son A.S.A.P. She cried on Mrs. Wright shoulder for half the night. She could use all the motherly love and moral support she could get, since she was holding a grudge and refused to speak to her own mother after allowing Tucker to take her son. After explaining the whole scenario to Epiphany's mom, she suggested Keisha get a police escort to help her retrieve her son. The next morning she did just that, but Tucker had a surprise for her. He handed the officer court papers. He already filed for temporary custody of their son citing abandonment on Keisha's part.

"Well ma'am there's nothing I can do," the officer said.

Tucker had already shut the door in their faces. Keisha wondered how she ever loved him. With the police standing right there she couldn't blackout, that would defiantly land her back behind bars. Having no other choice, she went home and cried her heart out to Tiara.

"The Lord would never put more on you then you could bear." Mrs. Wright sat on the bed next to Keisha with a box of Kleenex and her bible. "Maybe he was just a little unhappy with your behavior and this is just his way of getting your attention."

'God, Why are you doing this to me? I have nothing, no one,' Keisha would rather be dead then to live without her son.

Triple Crown Publications presents

CHAPTER 45

Smitty kept his word. Two hours after he left her at breakfast they met up and he had the 5g's for Shana. Surprised that he really came through, Shana was even more shocked that he was going so hard at the chance to fuck with Epiphany *again*. If that's what it took to get Raina out of jail and keep his ass off her back she would of hooked him up a long time ago. It was time to keep her end of the bargain. She dialed Epiphany, but after a few rings her voicemail picked up. Shana ended the call and dialed her back again still ending up with the same result—her voicemail. Smitty was starting to get a little uptight, thinking that Shana was trying to pull a fast one on him.

"Yo Sha, this is some bullshit. Just forget it, a'ight, gimme my shit back yo!"

"Yo nigga, pump your brakes. Damn, I already told her you feeling her so just take her number and holla at her later!"

"Nah fuck that, that wasn't the plan. You suppose to hook that shit up in front of me."

"Well, I can't do shit if she don't answer right!"

"Yo, that's why I'm saying, fuck it. Just gimme my loot back."

"Wait, I'm a keep trying until I get her then."

"Nah yo, I ain't got all fucking day!"

"Smitty, here just leave a message. I promise she'll call you back." Shana said passing him her cell phone, while it was ringing Epiphany's phone.

"Huh, what up ma, this Smitty. Holla back 917-555-2322, a'ight love."

"Now, was that hard?" Shana asked.

"Nah, but shorty better holla back else me and you gon' have a serious beef, word up!" Smitty threatened.

"Trust me, she'll call. Damn, what the fuck she did that got you so strung the fuck out nigga?" Shana was curious because Smitty was acting a little to desperate and nervous.

"Yo, she ain't do shit." Smitty answered hostilely.

"Whatever nigga, just hold on tight to your phone, so you don't miss her call. Oh and here's her cell number just in case."

"A'ight, stop talking shit and hurry up and get Raina out for she bust that ass." Smitty laughed taking the piece of paper from Shana. Shana ignored his snide remark, but that's exactly what she was on her way to do—post Raina's bail and be out. As she started up her car and pulled off she tried dialing Epiphany again just to see if she'd answer, and this time she did.

"Hello?"

"Oh, now you answer." Shana said sarcastically.

"Girl, I'm sorry, I was on the phone with my boo and the shit he was talking was sounding too good to be put on hold. But anyway, what's good?" Epiphany said.

"Well damn, I'm glad my life didn't depend on you answering your phone and what's good is the same shit we already talked about. Unless your *boo* got you having a change of heart."

"You know what, Shana, I'm in a good mood right now, so I'm not even gonna entertain your smart ass, a'ight?"

"Yeah, okay. Just check your message and hit that nigga back!" Shana demanded and abruptly ended the call.

'Ooooh I can't stand that bitch.' Epiphany retrieved Smitty's message and phoned him.

"Yo, who this?" Smitty wasn't familiar with the number.

"Who you been expecting?" Epiphany said in a sensual tone.

"Yo, don't play games, who this?" Smitty asked again. Even though he assumed it was Epiphany, he ain't want to seem like he was beasting.

"Damn, my feelings is hurt. I thought you was waiting on my call."

"C'mon Ma, you know I been waiting to talk to you, what up though?"

"I don't know, my girl, Shana, told me that you was checking for me?"

"Yeah, you don't remember me?" Smitty questioned.

"From where?"

"I don't know, around I guess. But yo, that's neither here nor there. I'm trying to see you, ma."

"Not a problem!"

"Cool, I'ma call you later at this number when I'm ready to scoop you, a'ight."

"No doubt, see you then!"

CHAPTER 46

All Shana did was post Raina's bail. She didn't care how the girl got home, or if she even had money to get home, but as far as she was concerned her part was done. Shana was actually relieved now that she felt her and Smitty had resolved their issues and once she paid him back she was no longer in debt to him. The Chasity drama was dead and with Raina bailed out all the skeletons in her closet where gone.

"Yo Sha, this bullshit gotta stop between us." K.C. said as soon as she walked in the apartment.

"Stop what K.C., your lying or your cheating?"

"Come on, baby, how long you trying to be mad at a nigga?"

"K.C., you know what, right now you better be glad all I'm doing is giving you the silent treatment, cause I could go out and get me a nigga that knows how to treat a bitch. Instead, I stay stuck like glue to your muthafucking ass and what do you do? Nothing, but talk shit, lie and bring fucking diseases home."

"Disease? Yo, what you mean disease? Ain't nothing wrong with my dick?" Since K.C. had no symptoms, he had no idea what she was talking about.

"Oh nigga, you ain't go get your dick checked, yet? That's right, d-i-s-e-a-s-e muthafucka. You know, the shit you get when

197

you out in the streets fucking nasty hoes with no condom." Shana sarcastically yelled.

"Yo, I don't know what you talking about. I supposedly gave you something, what I give you huh? K.C. didn't have a clue.

"Nigga, you gave me Chlamydia from being out there with other bitches. Play stupid if you want to, but you better hope my other tests come back negative."

"Yo, I ain't never heard of that, but if I did I'm sorry. I ain't fucked around on you in a minute though. Sometimes I think something's wrong with me, like maybe I got the same shit that Halle Berry's man got. I don't know why I be fucking other bitches–I just do. I'm a go get my shit checked out, so can you stop being mad at me please." K.C. always had a way with words and as much as Shana didn't want to fall victim to his bullshit, she couldn't help it. She suffered from a sickness called love, she just loved him. She didn't know why, but she did. He was always able to break her down, and love was stronger than pride. Shana forgave him, but only on one condition—her tests had to come back negative.

CHAPTER 47

On his way to meet up with Epiphany, Smitty couldn't help but feel a little nervous about fucking with her again. Especially after the way he dogged her the first time. It was like she had some kind of hex on him because even after getting stomped out in public by C-God and Mike, over her, he still sort of obsessed over her. Honestly, he regretted forcing himself on her and wanted another chance with her. Epiphany wasn't comfortable with Smitty picking her up from her parents home, so she arranged for him to meet her at this cozy little Cuban restaurant on Queens Boulevard. She waited for him to arrive, so they could go in and be seated together. The dimly lit restaurant was small, but always packed. The tables were so close together, it almost felt like people were sitting on top of each other, but for some reason no one seemed to mind. There was a long period of silence between the two. Epiphany stared at Smitty often, her intent looks made him a little apprehensive, but she couldn't help it because something about him seemed all to familiar.

"I'm sorry I keep looking at you so hard, but there's something about you—I just don't know what it is." Epiphany said breaking the silence first.

"Stop trying to figure it out and let's just have a good time. We could start by ordering some drinks." Rudely, he flagged down the waiter. Epiphany ordered a apple martini and since Smitty was feeling the guilt eat away at him he ordered a

Greygoose mixed with Hennessy and a splash of cranberry juice to help mellow him out. The alcohol did ease the tension a bit, as the two began to converse a little more. Smitty complimented everything from Epiphany's hairstyle to her shoes and also ran a few dry jokes by her. Epiphany chilled on the hard looks and pretended to find his jokes funny. After dinner Smitty wasn't ready to call it a night just yet, so he suggest that she following him to this little bar on Linden called Deja' vu. But, all Epiphany could think about was getting home in time for her midnight call from Wild. She tried to refuse, but ended up giving in to his pleas and agreed to go and have one drink. When they walked inside the bar, they both stopped to check out the pictures posted up on the wall from the previous parties held there and from the looks of it everybody seemed to be having a great time. As the two took a seat at the bar, Epiphany glanced around to check out the spot. She could tell it had a nice vibe to it and since the crowd looked to be a mature one, there wasn't a lot of rowdiness. The bartender was very friendly as she took their drink orders and Smitty went on to boast to Epiphany about a popular book the bartender wrote entitled "Sheisty." Nevertheless, Epiphany didn't find that to be all that impressive, but she did like the way the girl made her apple martini strong.

One drink ended up turning into three as they both started to unwind around one another. Epiphany had to admit it, his jokes got better and so did her liking for him (after the alcohol kicked in, of course). Smitty was doing his best to keep her entertained, hoping that his jokes mixed with the strong ass drinks would land him up in the pussy again, only this time not by force. Unfortunately for him, that thought was more of a pipedream, 'cause yeah he might have been given a second crack at her but, the game was still the same as far as Epiphany was concerned. Her goodies stayed in the jar until a nice amount of money had been spent. It was gonna cost him a little more than a meal and some drinks to taste her cookie. As soon as 11:30 hit, Epiphany decided to call it a night, leaning over she planted a soft kiss on his lips.

"Goodnight."

'*Damn,*' he thought, caught a little off guard as the softness of her lips and the whiff of her scent, which made his dick rise.

"You leaving me already?" Smitty questioned with disappointment.

"Yeah I have to go. I finally recognize where I know you from though." Epiphany said.

"What?" Smitty responded tensely as his heart began to pound.

"Yeah, I remember you now, from Club Cream a while back. You were at the bar with K.C. and some other guy."

"Oh yeah okay, right…right!" Smitty answered as he let out a deep sigh of relief. He didn't know how he was gonna to fuck with Epiphany without the torture of worrying about when, or if she would ever remember how much she really hated him and why. As Epiphany left, Smitty waited for a few moments and then secretly followed her to her home for the hell of it.

CHAPTER 48

A couple weeks passed and things were all good between Shana and K.C., especially since her test results came back negative. She even escorted him to the clinic to get tested. Since K.C. knew he was running around fucking everything insight, he took it a step further and agreed to be tested for HIV. Shana still refused to take one because she felt that since his results came back negative then she was negative and HIV was as simple as that.

Shana was also able to relax more without the static from Raina. Maybe Raina wasn't upset about having to stay in jail a couple of days and was just happy to be home, so she decided to let it go. K.C. and Smitty were still handling their business, money would soon be straight for them. Now Smitty was all caught up in Epiphany, therefore K.C. and his friendship turned into more of just a business partnership. Of course, Shana was happy about that, because that meant K.C. ran the streets less and spent more time with her. They were finally starting to connect, they laid up for most of the day watching movies, making love, getting high and even talking about one day having kids. It all seemed to good to be true because in the three years that she's been with him all they ever seem to do was fight, fuss and fuck. Sure he claimed to love her, but this was the first time since his bid that she actually felt his love for her. She felt the time was right to clear her conscience and pull all her skeletons out of the closet. She told him that her and C-God had more then just a business relationship, but it was brief, she then went on to drop what she thought was going to be a bomb–her sexual experience with Chasity. To her surprise K.C. already knew, he said he had got the word on all that when he was locked up.

"How?" Shana questioned, anxious to know the answer and hoping it wasn't Smitty that told.

"Yo, don't worry about it , just know in jail a nigga hear everything!"

"Well, was you mad when you heard?"

"What I'ma be mad for? Baby girl, you was holding a nigga down, so how I'm a knock your hustle. The shit about you fuck-ing with that bitch, man, I knew as soon as daddy came home that shit was gon' be a wrap!" K.C. said.

For the first time in a long time Shana was able to exhale. She was glad to know that she didn't have to stress over none of her secrets anymore, but she also was mad that Smitty put a twenty-thousand dollar dent in her pocket for nothing. K.C. caught Shana gazing off into a deep thought.

"Yo, is there something else you gotta to tell me?"

"Nah, that's it." Shana smiled and snapping out of her trance.

"A'ight then, climb up on daddy's dick and give me some of that pussy." K.C. ordered. Shana was more then happy to obey his order. Just as she was about to lay it down there was a hard knock at the door.

"Who the fuck is that knocking like they crazy? Oh boy, I bet it's Smitty's stupid ass," Shana said slightly raising her voice as if her high was just blown. She got up out of bed and threw on something to go see. Swinging open the door, expecting to see Smitty, she was surprised to find four policemen standing there. Her heart dropped. She knew it would be only a matter of time before she was busted.

"Shana Marie Scott, you're under arrest for the intent to sell and distribute drugs. you have the right to remain silent..." The arresting officer read her rights, handcuffed her and hauled her off to jail.

CHAPTER 49

Keisha was working hard to get her life in order. She was granted weekly unsupervised visits with her son until her court date for custody. After enrolling back in school part-time, she got a job at a real estate office working for commission. Lastly, she left *blackplanet.com* alone. Everything was starting to come together once she became a believer in Christ. Going to church and reading the bible with Mrs. Wright helped Keisha develop a better understanding about what it meant to believe in God. She's learned to stop blaming the Lord for her bad decisions and mess-ups because "although he is the Almighty," her pastor would say "sin is your choice."

Changes didn't happen over night, so when thoughts of killing Lea surfaced in her mind every so often she just prayed for strength. Keisha refrained from having any kind of contact with Tucker, at least until the court hearing came. Momma D's house was the location for the baby's drop off and pick up, that way they never had to cross each other's path. When she was lonely and missed him so, she'd press *67 before dialing his cell just to hear him say 'hello'. And oddly enough, she felt he was doing the same because she had gotten quite a few crank calls herself. It was over between them and she was almost ready to move on.

Keisha had made amends with Loretta and started calling her 'ma'. The two of them talked on the phone everyday, sometimes twice a day, establishing a tight-knit relationship, discussing any and every thing on their minds. Loretta's discussions were mainly about her mistakes and Keisha's younger sisters. Keely, only 16, wasn't going to school and hanging out to all times if the night with the local thugs. Kelly was a breath of fresh air, attending Clark University and doing exceedingly well. Keisha would always be her mother's pride and joy, her first–born, her lovechild, and she expressed that love to her every chance she got. Keisha had to admit she loved feeling her mother's love and how blessed she was to have a second mom in Mrs. Wright. Keisha's improvement made Mrs. T proud. Keisha gave Mrs. Wright hope that her own daughter, Epiphany, would make a change in her life as well.

CHAPTER 50

Tucker was finally adjusted to Lea being around; she was loving, caring and very helpful with little man and he appreciated that more than anything else. Following his mother's death, every woman his father would bring home despised him and didn't want the responsibility of caring for another women's child, which lead to abuse. His father's need for women was much stronger than his need to be a dad, so he allowed the hateful behavior from them to go on without saying a word. Lea was such a good women to him and his son, he decided to take their relationship a step farther—with a 3-caret, emerald cut diamond and a marriage proposal. Yes, he was ready to take it there, but he didn't want a big blow-out wedding like the one he and Keisha were planning. No, this time, he wanted it to be simple without her feeling cheated so he planned to take her to Montego Bay Jamaica to tie the knot.

Sometimes, he wondered if maybe he should of just married Keisha. Things might have turned out differently and she would have been his wife. No matter how hard he tried to front, he missed what she was to him and deep down inside the love he had for her was still there. Clearly too much had happen to turn back.

Tucker phoned his boys down South to tell them the latest.

"Hey what's up cuz, you alright, dawg ?" Peewee recognized the New York number.

"Yo, I'm chilling Pee, how you?"

"Man, shit is all gravy thanks to you."

"Where my nigga, Cornell at?"

"Ay, T, man since that nigga done got a little paper in his pocket he stay fucking around with these scandalous ass broads down here man. I'm try'na get this paper dawg!"

"I hear that! But listen, man don't let no bullshit come between ya'll niggas. You know what I'm saying?"

"Nah dawg, never that, that nigga just a little off track. That's all it is, we good. But what up with that faggot ass dude, C-God man, he surface yet?"

"Nah, he still hiding. But yo, I just called to let ya'll niggas know, your boy gon' go head and jump the fucking broom!"

"Ay, T, man, that's what's up! Congrats on that dawg. Make your baby momma your wife, cousin." Tucker hadn't been in touch with Pee and Cornell in weeks.

"Nah, not me and Keish dawg. Her name's Leanne." Tucker said realizing how awkward the conversation just got.

"Ay dawg, I ain't even gon' touch that, but whatever happen musta been fucked up 'cause dawg you was in *love* with Keisha."

"Yeah man, I had to move on from that. This one's a nice one though."

"Congratulations on that then, cuz! How lil' man doing?"

"He's good, a that's them coming in now. Listen, tell Corn to holla at me and ya'll niggas stay tight. I'm a kick it with you soon, a'ight?" Tucker hung up the phone in a hurry, so he could build up the nerve to pop the question.

Lea returned from the park with lil' man in her arms. As soon as he saw his daddy, the baby started squirming, crying and fighting to get away from her. As soon as she put him down, he ran over and clutched onto Tucker like he was afraid of Lea.

"What's wrong with him?" Tucker picked up his son.

"I don't know, maybe something scared him at the park." Lea's excuse didn't sit well with Tucker. He never thought that Lea would do anything to hurt his son. Playing it safe he chose to hold off on asking *the question* for a little while.

CHAPTER 51

Epiphany was spending a lot of time with Smitty. If she was still interested in niggas making small time figures he could've actually won her heart—he accommodated her need to be spoiled. But, she wasn't trying to get caught up with him and lose focus on the plan. He was friends with the nigga that tried to kill her and more than likely he knew about it. Epiphany didn't know what it would take to persuaded him to kill Ness for her, but she decided it was time to let Smitty sample her goodies when she overheard a discussion he was having with K.C., concerning some conflict with Ness, she knew he was ready to sever all ties with him. Their beef would be the beginning of Ness' end.

Smitty started to develop strong feelings for Epiphany, however he was growing impatient and tired of doing all the whining, dining and spending for nothing. He never was that type of nigga to kick out cash for ass, but he was splurging like crazy and even though he already hit it once, he was thirsty to find out what it tasted like. *'Damn I guess you should never say never, but fuck it. I'm just gonna throw it out there and ask for some.'* Smitty picked up the phone and called to confirm their date.

"Hey Boobie." Epiphany answered.

"What up Ma, we still on for the night?"

"Oh, no question, why? Where you want me to meet you at this time?"

"Yo, why you always gotta meet me, why I can't just come pick you up?"

"Because."

"Because what, you don't trust me?"

"Smitty, it ain't about that. You know what happened. I just don't want to bring no bullshit to my parents house."

"Yeah a'ight, yo, I guess I gotta respect that. So meet me at the Holiday Inn at nine o'clock, a'ight."

"Ooooh, so does that mean I should bring something sexy to wear?" Epiphany said giving him all the assurance he needed. Before he could respond, her other line beeped. It was Wild. She rush him off "Nine o'clock is good, I gotta take this call. Bye." Epiphany switched over to Wild's.

"Damn I miss you, baby," she said seductively.

"For real? I miss you too. I miss you so much I followed you today." Epiphany's heart pounded rapidly.

"S-s-stop playing baby!" She stuttered.

"Yeah, I'm playing, but you saving that stuff for me right!"

"Oh, no doubt daddy. This pussy belongs to only the Wild One. When you coming for it?" she teased.

"As a matter of fact I'ma be back in town tomorrow after-noon. So what's up, you packing your bags, or what?"

"Hell yeah, I can't wait."

"A'ight, sweet sugar panties, I'll pick you up soon as I touch down around noon."

"Okay baby, as soon as you touch down." Epiphany repeat-ed.

"I got you," said Wild as he hung up the phone.

CHAPTER 52

K.C. rushed down to the precinct to see what was up with Shana. The arresting officers wouldn't disclose any information other than she was being brought up on felony charges. He took that little bit of info for what it was worth and immediately called his lawyer Mr. Loboski to explain the situation and ask if he'd take her case. His attorney agreed. K.C. considered calling Shana's mom, Ms. Pat, but she hated him and would definitely use this situation as an opportunity to badger him. That was the last thing he needed right now, especially since he had nothing to do with this mess Shana got herself into. The only thing left for him to do was go home and wait by the phone for Shana to called him.

After hours of interrogation, name calling and harsh threats, Shana managed to hold her head, she wasn't confessing to nothing. The police had some solid evidence against her. Not only did Raina drop dime, but her supplier's perverted ways finally caught up with him and he sang like a bird when the Feds nabbed him. Apparently, an underage girl accused him of drugging her and then trying to have his way with her. Raina also told the police that he was a big time drug dealer, which they already a suspected. Shana was not only concerned about her ecstasy ties with her supplier, but the police confiscated several security tapes from his house, some with her on them. Still Shana refused to talk, the only words she had for them were: "Can I make my phone call now?"

215

CHAPTER 53

C-God gave up on trying to get in touch with Reggie by phone; it was time to head back to the Big Apple and find his ass. C had already let shit ride long enough. Alpo was his number one supporter and he really wanted C-God to stop getting high, get himself together and take back what was rightfully his. Of course C-God loved the sound of that, so he was trying hard to stay clean, at least while handling business.

They rented a utility van, loaded it up with rope, duck tape, guns, Aplo's dog, Venom, and Hassan, one of the few ride or die niggas from VA. Being back in New York made C-God realize how much he missed it, but with the death of his parents, the end of his reign and everything else the city represented—greed, murder and betrayal—he vowed to never live there again. Before hitting the hood, C-God stopped by the cemetery to ask his mom and pop for forgiveness. He was sorry for all the misery that he caused them; their blood, sweat, tears and death. Next to his parents plots were his brothers, Paul aka 'Pop' and Russell aka 'Black' Hinderson. Dead for years, they never saw their baby brother's raise to the top. C-god wasn't religious but he knew they had to be watching over him and asked that they guide him through his mission and make sure he kept it straight gangsta. Having made his peace with the family it was time for revenge. Next stop, the hood!

After scouting out the projects a few times and all of his former spots, there was no sign of Reggie. C-God had no choice but to go by the nigga's crib. He carefully got out the van checking his surrounding and instructed Alpo and his boy to do the same. He walked up to the front door and rang the bell.

"Tanya, you back already?" Reggie's elderly grandmother asked as she slowly approached the door. C was confused. *"Did she just say Tanya?"* Still focused on finding Reggie, he didn't dwell on it.

"Nah, Mrs. Mattie, it's C. Is Reggie home?"

"C, C who? Nawl, he ain't home."

C-God didn't respond. He returned to the van, parked it two houses away and waited. Minutes later, Tanya drove up with his son, a bag full of groceries and a pot belly, looking about three or four months pregnant. C-God shook his head in disgust and pulled off realizing that was probably the reason why Reggie was avoiding him. To be honest about it, he knew he could never be what Tanya needed, even if he tried. He wouldn't have been mad if they, especially Reg, came to him with the truth instead of being sneaky. *'But fuck it, what's done is done,'* he thought.

Taking one more loop around the area, they decide to stop and get a quick bite to eat at the Philly Cheesesteak spot on Linden Boulevard. While C-God sat in the van, waiting for Alpo and Hassan to come out of the restaurant, a pearly white Range Rover blasting "Lean back" pulled up right in front of him. What do you know, fuck finding Reggie, out jumped the head nigga in charge-Ness, who headed for the store next door to the eatery. C-God smiled. His brothers up in ghetto heaven must of been listening.

"Yo, God what the fuck you smiling at man?" Alpo asked as he and Hassan got back in the van.

"Yo, guess who just hopped the fuck out that truck, right in fucking front of me." C-God said.

"Get the fuck out of here, you sure that's that nigga," Alpo questioned.

"Hell yeah, that's that muthafucka Ness. He in the store right now."

"Yo Hassuan, gimme my shit." Hassuan handed Alpo his gun. Yo, I'ma go hop in that muthafuckas backseat, a'ight! Ay, C-God, pull up in front of the nigga's truck. I'll make sure he follows you." Alpo pulled his black hoodie over his head, crept up to Ness' car, opened the back door, climbed in and waited for him.

CHAPTER 54

Epiphany arrived at the Holiday Day Inn at 9:05 pm. She pulled into a vacant parking spot and took a couple of minutes to apply a little more gloss to her already shiny lips in her rearview mirror. Before getting out the car, she clutched down on the bottom of her Fendi bag to make sure she had her 22. She made it a priority to never leave the house without it after her near death experience. Normally, she would have had her nine, but it never turned up after *that* night. For her having some protection was better then none at all, she would say *'a 22 might not kill a Muthafucka, but it will defiantly complicate their intentions to harm me.'* Covering all areas, she was ready for whatever and had her game face on as she pranced towards the hotels entrance, where she found Smitty waiting. Inside their room, Epiphany wasted no time getting down to business. Opening her little over night bag, she pulled out something more appropriate for the occasion. She suggested Smittty order a bottle of champagne from room service, preferably Veuve Clicquot, while she showered and slipped into something sexy for him. Smitty liked the idea of her slipping into *'something sexy.'* The hood rats he used to fuck with considered a matching bra and panties set 'something sexy', if he was lucky.

The champagne arrived just before Epiphany opened the steamy bathroom door. Smelling so fresh and so clean like cucumber melon in her red lace Vickie Secret lingerie number, Smitty was mesmerized. Holding two glasses of bubbly, the bulge in his boxers was starting to show and he wondered if she tasted as good as she smelled. Seductively, she walked over to him, removed both glasses from his hands and one by one took both of them straight to the head. Epiphany placed the empty glasses down, pushed him onto the bed and slowly climbed on top of him, gliding her tongue across his chest. Smitty's eagerness wouldn't allow him to just lie there and enjoy her foreplay, he wanted Epiphany, now. Flipping her over, he ripped her panties off and aggressively started licking her pussy. Epiphany squirmed from discomfort as he licked and sucked on her with such brute force. She tried to move his head from between her legs, only Smitty continued like some kind wild beast in a trance; pinning her legs down to the bed and ignoring her screams for him to stop. His behavior struck a cord. Suddenly, Epiphany flashed back to why she hated him in the first place. She remembered him raping her. In a panic she began to gasp for air. Hysterical, she punch him repeatedly, finally getting him to stop. She jumped up from the bed, grabbed her purse and ran in the bathroom. Locking the door behind her she quickly dumped out her bag, searching for her asthma pump. Calming down after a few minutes she sat on the bathroom floor, holding her gun in her hand. Meanwhile Smitty stood on the other side of the door, begging for her forgiveness.

"I'm sorry, baby. I don't know what got into me. Please give me another chance. I really care about you, Epiphany. Come out, we'll just lay down—no sex—I promise."

It was too late. Epiphany wanted to shoot him through the door, but as badly as she wanted to kill him she knew she had to see Ness suffer first. She put her gun away, pushed her feelings to the side, opened the door and laid in Smitty' arms, awake for the rest of the night.

CHAPTER 55

"Shut the fuck up, keep your eyes on the fucking road and lets follow that van, muthafucka." With Alpo's piece pointed at his head, Ness had no other choice but to follow his orders.

C-God lead them to an abandoned house way out in Far Rockaway, where the torture began. Ness, scared shitless, parked his Range behind the unmarked van in the driveway. Hassan hopped out the van with his Uzi ready to shoot and instructed Ness to get out slowly.

"Yo, what the fuck is going on, man? What the fuck ya'll niggas want with me? Here, take the fucking truck and let a nigga go, yo. What ya'll niggas want money, too? Let me call my man, have him bring as much as ya'll want." Ness's pleas went ignored. The car keys and roll of hundreds he threw at his kidnappers laid right where they fell, on the ground.

"Shut the fuck up nigga! This ain't about no truck or no money, you rat bastard muthafucka." Hassan patted Ness's down for weapons.

"Move it you bitch ass nigga, get in the house." Alpo said.

"Hell no, , if ya'll niggas is gon' kill me, do it right the fuck here 'cause I ain't going inside that house." Ness said boldly.

"What muthafucka!" said Alpo and Hassan. They pushed

him to the ground and started kicking and pistol whipping him. "Nigga, ain't nobody giving your punk ass a choice," yelled Alpo. Hassan grabbed Ness by his feet and started dragging him towards the house.

"Ahhhhh..." Ness yelled out in agony from the burning sensation of his flesh ripping across the concrete. Once inside the house, they stomped him out again and tied him to an old chair that a crackhead probably brought in to use. Staring through half shut eyes and into the faces of Alpo and Hassan, Ness tried to figure out where he might of knew them from, but neither one of them seemed familiar. He wondered if this was pay back for murdering that kid Righteous, or maybe just some hating ass niggas that heard about the paper he was getting. All of his questions were answered when C-god walked in.

"Well, well, well, what up, sheisty ass nigga?" C-God taunted.

Ness didn't recognize C-God at first, once a buff dude, crack made him lose over fifty pounds. If Ness hadn't of remembered C-God's voice, he might have never figured out who he was.

"Oh shit C, that's you nigga? Look like you could use a meal or two. What the fuck you doing, getting high? Damn nigga, I'm disappointed in you." Bloody, bruised and facing death, Ness was still a smart ass.

"Fuck you muthafucka, you should of killed me when you had the chance 'cause a nigga came back just for your punk ass. Yo, Alpo bring your dog in since this nigga got a thing for dogs!" C-God demanded. He planned on having Venom bite into Ness's flesh while he washed the wounds with ammonia.

"Nah nigga, that's your baby moms." Ness sarcastically referred to C's baby mother sucking off a pit bull to get some free drugs. C-God had been disrespected enough by this guy, but he couldn't believe that Ness had the balls to be tied up with no where to run out in Far-ass-Rockaway and still continue to pop shit. C-God rushed Ness, jabbing his stun gun right into his chest.

"Tape his fucking mouth up," C ordered Hassuan. After a night filled with torture, C-God was ready to end it once and for all. For the grand finale C-God, Alpo, and Hassan placed Ness in a barrel filled with lye and watched while he helplessly hollered and squirmed as is skin burned away.

CHAPTER 56

Keisha picked up her son bright and early from Momma D's house. She had a wonderful day planned and wanted to get an early start. During their visit, she noticed bruises on his upper right arm like someone had squeezed or punched him really hard. Furious, she began to further inspect his body, finding another identical bruise on his thigh. *'Oh hell no!'* Right away she knew Lea was abusing her son and there was no way she would allow him to spend another second with that monster. Outraged, Keisha called Tucker's cell phone and went off on him as soon as he answered.

"Wait calmed down a minute, I can't understand a word your saying, Keisha."

"*I said*, have you seen these fucking bruises on our son? Tucker he's not coming back to that house as long as that bitch is in it. She better hope to God I never see her."

"What are you talking about bruises, what bruises?"

"On his body Tucker! Listen to me, Lea's playing you like she played me. I thought she was my friend, but she set me up and confessed to it after she had me arrested."

"What?"

"Lea drugged me the night of my party and sent you tha

tape. She told me how she wanted to get with you and how you shut her down 'cause we were together. Anyway, what's done is done, I don't give a fuck about none that anymore. She got you and that's fine but little man is another story. If you don't keep her away from him, I swear before God, I'm gonna hurt her."

"Keish, are you still at Momma D's house."

"No, I'm at Epiphany's?"

"Well can you please come outside, I'm on my way." Tucker remembered his son's behavior towards Leanne a couple of days ago.

As soon as Keisha stepped out the front door with her son Tucker was pulling up in front of the house. Hopping out the car, he ran straight to lil' man to see what Keisha was ranting about.

"Tucker, she did this," she said pulling up the baby's sleeve, "I know she did this. When I called you after I got out of jail, she was real loose with her mouth. She asked if I was calling to speak to *'her man'* or my *'fucking rugrat brat'*. That's why I tried to come get him, but you pulled that custody stunt and now look at his arm and his leg. I'm telling you T, she wants to get rid of lil' man like she got rid of me. Just think, if Lea can drug me, pay a guy to have sex with me, taped it and send it to you, there's no telling what else she's capable of." Keisha was hysterical.

Tucker listened without saying a word, everything Keisha was saying made a lot of sense to him. It was ironic that Lea came back into his life just as shit fell apart between he and Keisha. *'If she sabotaged my relationship ,than Keisha's right, what else...'* Tucker couldn't even finish his thoughts. He looked at the marks on his son again and his blood boiled.

"Keisha, I'll be back a'ight."

"Tucker, have you been listen to anything I just said?"

"Yeah and I believe you." Tucker got back in his 745 and sped off.

When Tucker reached home, Lea was in the kitchen trying her best to cook, but the burning smell that lingered throughout the house told a different story.

"Oh, hey honey." Lea said excitedly, when she spotted Tucker standing it the doorway of the kitchen.

Tucker gave her a fake smile. During his drive back to the house, his first thought was to fuck her up, but since Lea liked to play games he decided to play one on her.

"Ummm, smells interesting" He said.

"I know honey, I wanted to make you some breakfast, but it didn't turn out so great. Maybe we should go and get some take out again. I'm sorry!" Lea said in a disappointing tone.

"It's all good. Listen, let me kick it with you for a minute." Tucker took Lea by her hand and lead her to the living room couch. "Lea, I've been thinking about just letting Keisha go ahead and take full custody of lil' man. I know he's a handful and with you in school and everything, I just don't feel it's fair to you to have to take care of my son when he's Keisha responsibility." Tucker wanted to see where her head was at.

Lea's face lit up without smiling.

"Well honey, you know lil' man is a handful, but I don't mind looking after him. However, I think he does need to be with his mother. He misses Keisha, that's why I think he doesn't like me."

"Yeah, maybe your right, 'cause I know lil' man can make you wanna to knock the shit out of him sometimes, right?" Tucker chuckled then got serious. "Right, Leanne?" He asked again, looking her dead in the eye.

"No, I would never do that." Lea answered nervously.

"You wouldn't, are you sure about that?"

"Of course I'm sure, what are you getting at?"

"I'm getting at the fact that your not the only one that knows how to set up a hidden camcorder. That's right don't look sick in the face now. I saw you! I got you on tape hitting on my son." Tucker lied to get her to confess.

"Tucker wait hear me out, I can explain that. I didn't even hit him hard, I was just teaching him some discipline-"

"Lea, just go upstairs, get your shit and get the hell up out of my house. A'ight!" Tucker didn't want to hear her bullshit.

"Tucker please, don't!" Lea cried. Tucker let out a hard sigh, jumped up from the couch and yoked her up from the couch by her neck.

"Don't what? You violated when you put your hands on my son and that shit you did to Keisha was foul. Either you gon' get your shit and go, or leave it for the trash, but you better decide quick and trust me when I tell you this is me being nice!"

Lea's eyes watered from the tight grip Tucker called 'being nice'. When he let Lea go, she was shook, so shook that she left her all her belongings behind, grabbed her car keys and got the fuck up out of there. She knew she could never be his number one.

CHAPTER 57

Epiphany thought about what happened between her and Smitty the entire night. Allowing herself to be in his company again, sickened her. She didn't feel comfortable playing this little game anymore. All type of thoughts started to cross her mind, mainly that maybe she was the one being played. *'Smitty almost raped me a second time last night and Ness tried to kill me, shit maybe their scheming to finish me off'*. Finally, thinking sensibly, Epiphany felt seeking revenge this way didn't seem so sweet or safe for her anymore and it certainly wasn't worth losing her life over (for real this time). She eased Smitty's arm from around her, got out of bed and quietly put her clothes on. Before sneaking out, Epiphany gathered up all Smitty's belongings including his cell phone and took them with her. Inside her car she emptied out his pockets: $180 dollars in crumbled up twenties, a Cartier watch, platinum chain with a diamond studded Jesus head medallion, a wallet with nine crisp $100 dollar bills and his license. Epiphany started up her car and pulled off, reaching halfway home she smiled to herself. *'Payback is a bitch!'* She stopped at a gas station and tossed the useless possessions—his clothes, sneakers, empty wallet and phone— in a dumpster.

Strolling in the house, Epiphany was so excited to see her godson and Keisha together. She picked him up and held him tightly and he patted her softly on her back.

"Ooh it's so good to see you lil' T. I can't believe how big h‹

got Keisha." Epiphany kissed his cheeks. This was the first time she had seen him since she'd been home from the hospital.

"I know, they were feeding my baby well in ATL." They laughed and so did lil' T. " E, I thank you for making me realize that my son is my life. So much has happen and part of it was because of my stupidity and the other part, girl you wouldn't believe it if I told you."

"What?" Epiphany asked.

"We'll talk later, but since you're finally home for a change why don't you take us for a ride to get some breakfast."

"Damn, I would love to Keish, but I have to start packing."

"Packing what, where you going? You just got home.

"Packing my shit, girl, I'm moving to Jersey with Wild."

"The music producer?"

"Um hum, and by the way, where's my parents ?"

"Damn E, see that goes to show that you ain't never home 'cause you don't never know what's going on. Tiara and Jay when on a three day Gospel cruise.

"Gospel cruise! Pops must of finally gave in." Epiphany said in shock.

"Yeah, church is not so bad, you know."

"Oh God, not you, too, Keish?"

"Epiphany don't knock getting saved until you try it. Can I use your car while you pack?" Epiphany paused for a moment and wondered how her mom managed to turn everybody holy.

"Unbelievable," she mumble as she handed Keisha her car keys.

"Thanks, we won't be long." Keisha took lil' man from Epiphany arms and headed out the door. Epiphany rushed to the basement and started packing. Far in back of one of her drawers, she found some photos of herself, Keisha and Shana from the old days, when their clique was inseparable. *'Now Keisha's a mommy, Shana's married and I'm finally getting out of Southside Jamaica'*. Deep down inside she was going to miss her hood, but she vowed she'd never come back there to live. The house phone rang, Epiphany thought about not answering it, but assumed that it might be her parents calling so she decided to pick up.

"Wright residence."

"You have a call from *"Ramel"* at a correctional facility. To decline the call please hang up, If you except dial 5 now," said the recording. Epiphany rolled her eyes and hung up. A few minutes later it rang again, and she excepted the call.

"Hello, what happen?" Ramel said wondering why the phone cut off.

"Nothing happened" Epiphany said coldly.

"Epiphany!"

"Yeah."

"Oh shit what up, babygirl? I finally caught up with you. I been trying to holla at you for a while now, but you don't never be home. How's everything; you alright?" After Ramel had move out of her parent's house years back, him and Epiphany did their best to avoid each other.

"I was until now!"

"Yo, listen Epiphany, I'm sorry for that foul shit I put you through. Damn you don't know how much that shit fucks with me everyday, especially now that I got a little girl. I hate myself for that nasty shit, I know I violated you in the worst way and you never told on me as many time as you threatened to, you didn't. Hello, you there?" Ramel was uncertain she was there 'cause she had been so silent.

"I'm here." Tears started to run down her face.

"Oh, a'ight, just making sure. But listen, that's my time I just wanted you to know that I'm sorry. I love you and please be careful out there on them streets. Oh and between me and you, your pops and I searched hard looking for the nigga C-God. But, don't worry he'll surface one day and word is out in all the jails, so if he get lock up he's finished; dead just like the rest of his brothers." Ramel guaranteed her.

"Ramel, can you keep your eyes and ears open for this kid named Ness, he was the one that shot me. Oh and a cat named Smitty, he was down with it too."

"Ness, oh word he was the trigger man! I'm hearing alotta bad shit about that kid. He done already signed his death certificate when he kill that cat from Lefrak. He won't be breathing to much longer, but the other cat, I got you. A'ight, babygirl, I gotta go though please take of yourself."

"I will and thanks *Uncle*."

Uncle Ramel smiled because in his heart he knew Epiphany's last words meant that she forgave him. She stopped calling him uncle years ago.

CHAPTER 58

Shana's heart sunk when the *"fat cracker bastard"* denied her bail and adjourned her case for thirty days, suggesting that she utilize the time to adjust her attitude problem. She turned to her lawyer, with a *'do something'* look, but Shana(coming up in the court room rolling her eyes and sucking teeth before the judge) made it difficult to do anything. As she was being escorted back to the cell, Shana turned to K.C.

'Damn, I knew her attitude was gon get her in trouble one day'. K.C. shook his head in disappointment.

Shana timed K.C. perfectly because as soon as he walked in the apartment she called. K.C.

"Yo," K.C. answered, rushing over to the phone.

"Hey K.C.," Shana said.

"Ain't no 'hey' Shana, what the fuck was all that attitude about, today? Don't you know fucking around with the judge like that, you only playing with your own freedom, dummy. You could have all the attitude you want with them fucking police, but you ain't never s'pose to fucking around with no judge. But I guess now you found that shit out the hard way, right?"

"Yeah I guess your right, but they had it in for me from door 'cause these cops in here already told me how it was go down. That's why I had an attitude." Shana explained.

"Regardless, you don't fuck around with the nigga that holds your freedom card."

"Well, do you think he'll let me out on bail my next court date?"

"Yo Sha, you disrespected a judge in his courtroom. So, I don't know? He might make you wait it out until your sentencing."

"Damn, I fucked up!"

"Yeah, that you did."

"Well I got to go now. I'll let you know my visitors schedule as soon as I know it, a'ight. I love you!"

"A'ight Sha, I love ya ass too and ay, keep your head up baby girl. Shit'll be okay!"

CHAPTER 59

Smitty jumped up out of his sound sleep when the hotel phone rang to inform him that it was check out time.

"Yo ma, you wanna go get some breakfast." Smitty thought Epiphany was in the bathroom, but when he didn't get a response he got up out the bed to find that she was gone and so was his things. "Damn, that fucking bitch!" he yelled out standing in just his boxers. He became even more vexed when he discovered that his cell phone was gone, too. He needed to call K.C. so he could bring him some clothes, but he didn't know the number by heart. He paced back and forth until he came up with an idea, *'I could call information and see if any Shana Scott is listed.* Luckily, she was and the operator gave him two listings. *'Please somebody be home.'* His heart pounded, impatiently awaiting an answer.

"Hello?" K.C. answered.

"Yo man, thank God your home!"

"Smitty?"

"Yeah man, yo I need you to bring me a pair of jeans and a shirt" Smitty looked around the room to see if his sneakers wer gone too. "Oh and some kicks, too, man."

"Yo, nigga what happened, where you at? K.C. question

"Man, I'm at the Holiday inn next to Kennedy Airport. Yo, that fucking bitch done robbed me for my shit and bounce on a nigga while I was sleeping. Thank God I valet parked 'cause the bitch probably would of took my car keys, too."

"Who?" K.C. laughed.

"Your fucking chick's homegirl. That bitch Epiphany." Smitty was real sour.

"Yo man, didn't I tell your ass to leave that shit alone? Nigga, see you don't listen." K.C. continued to laughed and rub it in.

"Nigga. that shit ain't funny, yo, and I bet Shana's trifling ass knew what that fuck was up all along. Where she at 'cause I need that bitch, Epiphany, number again so I can get my shit back."

"Yo, nigga, Sha ain't have shit to do with that, beside she got her own shit to deal with man. Five-o came, took my baby and locked her ass up. She gotta do thirty days before she could even go back to court for a bail."

"Word, that's fucked up! But man, you got her cellphone at the crib with you, 'cause I need homegirl's number, now. I'm ready to kill that bitch, man. She played me good, for real!"

"Yeah I got it, hold up." K.C. searched Shana's phone and recited both Epiphany's house and cell number to Smitty.

"Good looking out nigga. I'm in room 234, come see me!" Smitty hung up and immediately dialed Epiphany's cell.

Epiphany had just finished packing when she looked at the time and realized it was almost noon, which meant Wild should be out front shortly to pick her up. The closer it got to noon the more excited she became. Epiphany reached for her ringing cell phone in her purse and accidentally pulled out Smitty's chain, which she thought would be a nice gift for Wild. She grabbed phone and noticed the screen read *blocked*. Now normally didn't answer blocked calls, but she wasn't going to take any ces on missing Wild so she answered.

"Hello?"

"Yo, why you play me like that, that was some fucked up shit you did you know that, right?" Smitty said.

"What? Nigga get over it! What you thought I wasn't gon' remember what you did to me. Well, the jokes on you mutha-fucka. It was a game nigga, you can't possibly be that dumb to think that I would fuck with you knowing that your boy is the nigga that shot me and killed my boyfriend, or maybe you are. *'You act like your pussy is gold.'* You remember saying that to me the night C-God and Mike stomped your punk ass out. Well, you know what it must be because your stupid ass went hard for it this time. Unfortunately you've been punked, muthafucka!" Epiphany was filled with vindication as she slammed down the hood of her phone.

Smitty was steaming mad. Epiphany might have thought this shit is over, but this time he was gonna see to it the she pushed up daisies. *'Nobody gonna play me like that and live to tell it.'* He sat on the edge of the bed and waited for K.C. to bring him some clothes.

CHAPTER 60

Epiphany would have felt threatened if Smitty knew where she lived, but since he didn't, fuck him. Right after she hung up on Smitty, Wild called to say he was only fifteen minutes away, "so be ready." For sure Epiphany was ready, ready to put South Side Jamaica, Queens and all it's drama behind her. She wrote three notes for the people she loved.

Mommy,

I'm happy to see that you found a home in the church. Try not to worry too much, I'll be fine. I love you, oh and I promise I'll stay in touch.

Epee,

Daddy,

You know your my number one, I love you more than any-thing. I only hope I haven't disappointed you too much I know you only want the best for me, so don't worry, I only want the best for me too! Try not to let the born again version of mommy drive you to drink. I'm just playing, I'm glad she got you into church. I'll be in touch.

Love always,

Epee,

Hey Keish,

I was hoping I'd get to see you before I left, I'm gonna miss you. You are my true friend and just because we don't have the same blood running through our veins don't mean we ain't real sisters. Take care of my godson and if you and Tucker don't get back together don't worry, it's his lost. You gotta promise me you'll come visited me soon. Tell Shana I said bye.

I love you!

Epiphany

P.S.

Keep the car.

By the time Epiphany finished her last letter her knight in shining armor was outside her house waiting for his princess. She took one final look around the house and headed to the door, where Wild's driver met her at the top of the stairs to carry her bags. Off to Jersey they went.

Keisha pulled up at the house seconds later, just missing Epiphany. She got out the car and opened the back door to take lil' man from his car seat.

"Hey E, I'm back," she yelled once she opened the front door. When Epiphany didn't answer she put her son down and noticed there were three folded pieces of paper on the kitchen table and one of them had her name on it. She read the letter and tears started to fall. Keisha was going to miss Epiphany and part of her knew she'd probably never see her friend again. Truth be told Epiphany, was good at starting over. Keisha could only hope that she wouldn't be forgotten. She called Tucker and he told her that he and Lea were over, he also apologized for being so fucked up towards her and wanted to know if they could try and make their family work. Keisha was hesitant for a moment, but more than any thing in the world she knew she wanted her family back together. She agreed, but only under certain circumstances.

"Tucker we can try again, but not in that house, not after Lea lived in it. I want us to start fresh." Tucker didn't see a problem with starting fresh at all. As a matter of fact when he went to get lil' man from Atlanta he loved it so much he purchased a six bedroom house on the low in hopes that maybe one day they would be united. He didn't tell her that part yet he figured he'd hold on to that bit of information and surprise her with it later.

"Whatever you want, Keish, I'm with you."

"Good, now me and lil' man would like to take you out."

"Sounds good. I'll be there to pick you up in a half." Tucker said.

"No, we're coming to get you, Epiphany gave me her rid

"Keish, I'm coming to get you. You don't need her car." After everything that went down, Tucker still disliked Epiphany.

"Tucker, stop it, we're leaving now. You don't have to ride in my new car. We'll switch when I get there, okay baby? It's not a big deal, alright!"

"A'ight and Keisha I want you to know that I never stopped loving you."

"Baby, I'm glad to hear that because I still love you, too. I'll see you when I get there!" Keisha said smiling.

Smitty spotted Epiphany's car pulling out as he turned the corner. Driving his black Expedition at full speed through the block he unloaded six shots from his nine through the driver's side window hitting Keisha. Realizing, all too late, that he shot the wrong girl, Smitty panicked and mashed down on the gas harder, losing control of the wheel, spinning across the street and crashing into a telephone pole. The impact knocked him out. A few of the neighbors witnessed the whole incident and called the police right away. Mr. Swinton, one of Jay Wright's buddies that lived next door, ran over to the car when he heard the baby's frantic cries and removed him from the back seat. Mr. Swinton checked his body to make sure he wasn't hit then told his wife to take him in the house away from the gruesome scene. In minutes the police and ambulance arrived but unfortunately Keisha was already dead.

Tucker called her cellphone several times wondering what was taking her so long, becoming a little worried he told himself that he'd try one more time before he headed over to pick them up. On his last try a police officer answered Keisha's phone and informed him that there had been a tragic accident and he needed to come right away. Tucker's heart dropped. Hearing the word *'tragic'* he automatically started to think the worst. Rushing over to Epiphany's house, he prayed to God, *"Please God not another one. Don't take another person I love away from me."*

As the ambulance carrying Smitty, who was in stable condi- pulled off, Tucker arrived at the scene and instantly broke down when he spotted Keisha's dead body lying on the ground next to the car door covered with a bloody sheet awaiting the coroner. It was heartbreaking to see him down on his knees holding her body, crying out in so much pain

"Keish, come on Keisha, please don't leave me, I need you baby!" He cried repeatedly. Tucker would give anything to bring her back.

Triple Crown Publications presents

THE FINAL CHAPTER

New Beginnings

It's been a year since Keisha was laid to rest in a Georgia cemetery and even though everyone's finally starting to move on she
will always be missed and never forgotten.

Tucker and lil' man moved down to Atlanta were they try to
make the best out of the situation, day by day. They found peace
in spending a lot of time with Keisha's mother, Loretta, grandmother and sisters Kelly and Keely, who has since straightened
up her act. On Sundays, besides having dinner together, they all
visit Keisha grave to bring fresh flowers. Tucker now counsels
youths about the negatives of the street gangs and the drug
game. Lil' man is growing so fast and looking more and more
like his mom everyday.

Shana served six months in jail and was released, but she
deeply regretted not being able to say goodbye at Keisha's funeral. She felt partly responsible for what happened. Because of her
own selfish reasons she hooked Smitty up with Epiphany. She
and K.C. are still together and things are good between them,
their little investment turned out to have a bigger profit then
expected. They were able to purchase a condo and opened
bar/lounge spot in Queens, called *Life*, that's doing well f
them. Although the money is straight K.C. still hustles. C
habits die hard. However, he did stop cheating and in

months he and Shana will be the proud parents of their first baby, *Keisha Shamari Cright*. It's a girl of course!

Smitty was brought up on murder charges and sentenced 15-to-life, but only lived to serve one month of his time. Uncle Ramel remembered the name and kept his promise. When Smitty was in Rikers, he had some of his people take care of him with a nice slit to the throat.

C-God stopped getting high and is back on the map in the never-ending drug game with his new partner Alpo. Together, can't nobody hold them down, that is as long as the Feds don't catch him.

Ness's remains were never found and only C-God, Alpo, Hassan and the dog Venom know why, and they're not telling.

Epiphany never made it to Keisha's funeral. She knew Tucker would blame her for Keisha death, just like he did with Malikai and she had to admit she blamed herself too. She felt she was supposed to die not them. If she had never invited Mali over to her house that night, or gave Keisha her car both of them would still be alive. The guilt ate away at her. She truly loved both of them dearly and does manage to visit their graves when she can. Her parents sold their house shortly after Keisha's death and moved to a nice area out in East Hampton Long Island, where her father, Jay Wright, and mother, Tiara, are both studying ministry and are devoted members to a new church.

Epiphany and Wild's moved to LA and shorty after their relationship started to deteriorate, it lasted for three months. Apparently, she felt he was *too nice*, she need drama in the relationship and since there was none, it got boring. Epiphany started hanging out at all the celebrity affairs and managed to meet the right people and get the exposure she wanted. *'It's not always what you know but who you know.'* Being with Wild for that short period of time served its purpose. Epiphany's now living lovely in Burbank California. She's dabbled in everything from modeling to dancing in videos, but her heart lies in acting. be on the look out for E.J. Wright's leading role in a independent film entitled *'SHEISTY'* coming soon …

ORDER FORM

Triple Crown Publications
2959 Stelzer Rd.
Columbus, Oh 43219

Name: _____

Address: _____

City/State: _____

Zip: _____

		TITLES	PRICES
		Dime Piece	$15.00
		Gangsta	$15.00
		Let That Be The Reason	$15.00
		A Hustler's Wife	$15.00
		The Game	$15.00
		Black	$15.00
		Dollar Bill	$15.00
		A Project Chick	$15.00
		Road Dawgz	$15.00
		Blinded	$15.00
		Diva	$15.00
		Sheisty ✓	$15.00
		Grimey	$15.00
		Me & My Boyfriend	$15.00
		Larceny	$15.00
		Rage Times Fury	$15.00
		A Hood Legend	$15.00
		Flipside of The Game ✓	$15.00
		Menage's Way	$15.00

SHIPPING/HANDLING (Via U.S. Media Mail)   **$3.95**

TOTAL $_____

FORMS OF ACCEPTED PAYMENTS:
Postage Stamps, Institutional Checks & Money Orders, all mail in orders take 5-7 Business days to be delivered.

ORDER FORM

Triple Crown Publications
2959 Stelzer Rd.
Columbus, Oh 43219

Name: _____

Address: _____

City/State: _____

Zip: _____

		TITLES		PRICES
		Still Sheisty	✓	$15.00
		Chyna Black		$15.00
		Game Over	✓	$15.00
		Cash Money		$15.00
		Crack Head		$15.00

SHIPPING/HANDLING (Via U.S. Media Mail)   **$3.95**

TOTAL $_____

FORMS OF ACCEPTED PAYMENTS:

Postage Stamps, Institutional Checks & Money Orders, all mail in orders take 5-7 Business days to be delivered.

Menage A' Trois

"MENAGE A' TROIS Sexy Flicks"
The Ultimate in Visual Entertainment

Experience visual entertainment at its best! Our photos of sexy ladies will take you far and beyond your imagination.

Order a Sampler Set today for only $9.99* + Shipping & handling $2.00
(Assortment of (10) Hot photos)
Send $2.00 for a preview Color Catalog+$2.00 shipping & handling
Send $6.00 for a multi-page Color Catalog-Includes Free shipping

Quantity	Item	Price
	"Sampler Set" (Assortment of (10) Hot photos)	$9.99
	Preview Catalog	$2.00
	Full Catalog (INCLUDES FREE SHIPPING)	$6.00
	Merchandise Total	
	Shipping & Handling	$2.00
	Total	

Send All Payments To:
MENAGE A' TROIS
2959 Stelzer Road Suite C
Columbus, OH 43219

*The Sampler Set is pre-selected
This is a limited time offer.

(As of January 2005)
*Free shipping & handling applies to full catalog orders only.